Schemes N Love

JOMI OYEL

First Published in Great Britain in 2024 by
LOVE AFRICA PRESS
103 Reaver House, 12 East Street, Epsom KT17 1HX
www.loveafricapress.com[1]

Text copyright © Jomi Oyel, 2024
All rights reserved.

No part of this publication may be reproduced, stored, or transmitted in any form by any means, electronic, mechanical, photocopying or otherwise, without the prior permission of the publisher, except in the case of brief quotations embodied in reviews.

The right of Jomi Oyel to be identified as author of this work has been asserted by them in accordance with the Copyright, Design and Patents Act, 1988

This is a work of fiction. Names, places, events, and incidents are either the products of the author's imagination or used fictitiously. Any resemblance to actual persons, living or dead, is purely coincidental.

---

1. http://www.loveafricapress.com

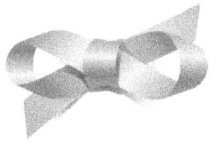

BLURB

Iyawa Jaseth, the life of every wild party and the queen of tipsy Instagram escapades, finds herself in a sticky situation. She's roped into a fake engagement with none other than the guy she can't stand, Matthias Bade.

Matthias only agrees to the sham to settle a debt, and Iyawa hatches a plan. She will make him fall head-over-heels for her, and then she'll shatter his heart. It becomes a wild challenge between the two.

But as the heat rises between them, the carefully constructed walls around Iyawa's heart begin to crumble. Could Matthias be the one to offer her the love she secretly craves? Or will her wild past be too much for him to handle?

Chapter One

Iyawa Jaseth had to agree with entrepreneur and financier Mitch Thrower when he said someone wasting your time was far worse than someone wasting your money.

And she was sure this man sitting in front of her was only going to waste her time. Was this the consequences of her rebelling? Ten minutes after she got her food, and she was already getting irritated.

"Hmm." He gave her a wink. "What do you say? Can I have your number?"

She puffed out as her gaze darted around the restaurant. Not much to see: red chairs and white tables, staff taking orders, people exiting the restaurant with white nylon bags.

The man leaned in. She turned her face to meet him and saw his hand land on hers.

Why in the world did he smell like he didn't use cologne? She withdrew her hand as fast as possible.

"Yeah, baby. You can pretend you can't hear me, but I'm not leaving 'til I get your number."

Her eyebrows set into a straight line as she had a sudden onset of nausea. *No, actually, she didn't hear him.*

The man reached for her other hand.

Iyawa rolled her eyes as she pushed it away. "Okay. Okay. Enough. Oh, I have had enough. Who are you again?"

The man shifted in his seat like he hadn't expected her to talk.

She studied him again. He'd dressed up like he was in a rock-and-roll band with metallic chains draped over his neck. How could this guy, who she didn't even know, walk over to her seat and ask for her number like this? What made him think they were compatible or something? She hated jewellery on men.

"The name is Paul. What happened, baby?" he asked, chewing his gum.

Iyawa frowned. Where in Ikeja did this man come up again? How couldn't he see she wasn't interested? *How can he be this desperate?*

"Okay, Peter. Just so you know, I'm not interested. I don't even know you. I just want to eat my jollof rice in peace, abeg."

The man's face pulled into a scowl. "The name is Paul. And I'm sorry if you couldn't eat because of me. I can't just leave yet."

She held her hand up. "I'm trying to be nice. I don't know you, and I don't want to. I don't do one-night-stands or whatever, so please, no number is coming from me. Please leave my table."

Paul's forehead creased. "Excuse me? I...I didn't say I'm interested in one-night-stands. I just want your number."

"And I said there is no need for it. I don't want to know you. Is that a problem?" Her voice was getting louder now.

Paul looked at the other diners who were now looking at him. "But... But I am—"

Iyawa shook her head. "You just came here expecting me to give you my number. Just like that. What effrontery? Do I look cheap?"

Paul rubbed his palms together and then—it seemed like he just couldn't contain it—he smirked.

"Oh, I know you well. You are that Iyawa Jaseth everyone is always seeing on the news. Aren't you the one who likes going to party and all?" he said with a wink.

Iyawa glared at him. She knew people in Ikeja wouldn't forget her past. She was naïve then. It'd been a year since she'd stopped her delinquent lifestyle, but people still liked to tag her to it.

"Leave my table before I shout. I can shout pretty well."

Paul scoffed, rising from the seat. "Whatever."

When he had left her table, she brought out a spray bottle from her purse and sprayed the content all in front of her, not paying attention to her food. Paul had been smoking, and she wasn't about to have his lingering scent remind her of what he'd just said about her past.

Good riddance to rubbish. What even was that, Iyawa?

Just then, her phone dinged with a text.

She reached for her reading glasses in her bag and put them on. She had been using reading glasses ever since she was eighteen. She was used to it but sometimes didn't like the weight on her nose.

Are you okay, Iyawa? Should I come to get you? It's almost 10 pm.

She contemplated whether she should reply. Her sister, Jadesola, would rush here any moment after the passionate argument she'd witnessed back at home.

She supported her head with her palm. This was all her father's fault. That man would seize any moment to cause an argument.

Iyawa switched off her phone. "Sorry, Jadesola. But this is my night. No distractions. I just want to have dinner."

She glanced around the restaurant. Some people were still looking at her. By now, she was sure they were beginning to recognize her. The celebrity who once got drunk, went live, and puked.

She tried to take a spoon out of her jollof rice but now, it smelled of her perfume.

Ah, what a waste. This is all Paul's fault.

The restaurant had looked so promising. One of the reasons why she loved Ikeja. Being the capital of Lagos and a popular city, it had beautiful restaurants and quite some views.

Maybe she'd made a good decision coming here, but now, she needed to get home. As they say, being alone at times isn't good for the mind.

Iyawa took a breath, staring at the entrance of the restaurant. Was she ready to go back home? She wanted to stay out late today, but her father would get angry. What kind of parent said such things to their child?

Her father had said she was acting like an unserious child just because she'd once had an addiction to partying and drinking. Iyawa birthed the headlines back in those days. Media tagged her the black sheep of her well-known tech family while her sister, Jadesola, was called the successful one.

They had been in the car in the parking lot at home, all three of them—her, Jadesola, her father—and her father had been complaining to his driver about how Iyawa's past would one day come to haunt him and leave him with shame.

She had been so embarrassed. They had just been coming from the office. Why did he have to bring her up after the long day at work? She wanted to rest, not to deal with this.

With the driver listening, she couldn't just let it go. Her Popsi had to stop airing her dirty laundry in the public. When the driver made the mistake of glimpsing at her through the mirror, she hadn't known what got into her to shout back at her father. She didn't even remember what she had said, but it sure got her father angry.

"Don't you dare use that tone when speaking to me!" he had said when he'd climbed out of the car.

"Tell me something, Popsi. How do you expect me to behave when you keep talking about me in front of our staff? What do you want from me? Don't you ever give up? Leave me alone. I don't even drink and party anymore."

Her Popsi never liked it when she raised her voice, but she wasn't even prepared for what came next.

"You never listen. God, you are such an unserious, stupid child. Not like your sister!"

Iyawa had stared at him in shock. She couldn't believe her ears.

Yes, there were so many things about her mother he wasn't so glad about. Something he made sure to always tell her while growing up.

But it wasn't like things weren't mutual between them both, so how dare he? Only her mother had a right to say this, since she was the one who'd carried her for nine months. He didn't.

He had no right at all. Even when Jadesola stood up to their father, she couldn't still believe he saw her as a mistake.

Iyawa might not remember so much about her mother, but she was sure they didn't view her as a mistake.

Her father's expression had relaxed a bit, but the old man had still gone on.

"I don't know why you make me say things. Why can't you just be like Jadesola?"

Those familiar words haunted her. *I am not Jadesola. I'm a different, Popsi. You just can't see it*, she'd wanted to say, but her mouth couldn't form any words. Her feet glued to the spot, she could only stare at her father.

All her life, she'd stayed away from arguments with her father. She didn't even know why he had brought up her issue. She had silently prayed to God not to let her die from a broken heart.

"Popsi, that is just too cruel. I don't like how you talk to my sister. Can you just let her be?" Jadesola had replied, her eyes twitching with annoyance.

That image of Jadesola and the maids looking at her with so much pity made her tummy clench and her blood boil. She hated that look. No one was to look at her with such empathy. She knew she might be a disappointment to him, and maybe she would never be like Jadesola, but no one should give her such a look.

Those words he said to her that night? Something a parent should never say. He'd crossed the line.

It wasn't like she really enjoyed her past coming to haunt her. Yes, she was once wild. But that was all gone now. Then, it had just been the only thing to make her feel good. The only thing to make her feel better about herself.

But no one had the right to call her a mistake. God didn't view her as one.

"You know what, Popsi? I'm out." Those were the words she'd managed to say before she'd stormed off.

She hung her head and sighed. The only thing he could do was shut her bank account like he always did. Fair punishment.

Her phone would be filled with messages from Jadesola assuring her their father meant nothing he'd said. Iyawa loved her half-sister. They might not have been on good terms—sisters with different mothers could be pitted against one another; Iyawa knew this from seeing her college friends' strained relationship with their half-sisters. But she couldn't hate Jadesola, even if she had wanted to. They had been best friends since they were young. Where Iyawa had been the stubborn, reckless child, Jadesola was just the sweetest. Jadesola, when she was younger, had once cried because she didn't like the way Iyawa and her father argued. She had always had this dream of a perfect family. Poor girl.

Sometimes, Iyawa agreed with her father. Jadesola was really the perfect, gentle, and brilliant child, and she was a mess. She wasn't really surprised when he named her the company's president. Something that should have been Iyawa's position. The first-born's job.

Her father hadn't really given her a position yet. She just worked for the betterment of the company.

Jadesola. Her sister would be so worried if she came late. Right. No point wallowing here all night. She got up from her seat and sashayed her way to the counter, her hips swaying with grace, her black high-heeled shoes completing her signature look.

She could hear some men arguing over the last Champion's League match and some ladies laughing in another corner of the restaurant.

And as soon as they noticed she was looking, they all stared at her. Her dark hair stood out in long waves over her shoulder, with loose curls caressing her face.

At the counter, a staff came up to her.

"Can I pay my bill now?"

The female staff placed a neat glass back into the arranged glass rack and turned to Iyawa with a smile. "Yes, of course. Cash or card?"

Iyawa returned her smile. "Card, please. That would be POS, right?"

"Yes, ma'am."

As soon as she had gotten her receipt, she turned to go but was stopped by the staff.

"Sorry, but you look really familiar, and I can't place where I've seen you."

Iyawa tried smiling.. "I am Iyawa Jaseth.. My father's company make those popular phones everyone call TeleSparks. You must have seen me on the television."

Her Popsi's telecommunications company, TeleInc, was a Nigerian electronics and mobile company in Ikeja. TeleInc had expanded to over twenty countries so she was a little surprised this woman didn't quite know her.

The woman shook her head as her eyes widened. "Yeah. Your video, I am sorry about it. Trust me, I know it's not easy to vomit in public."

Iyawa managed a smile. Everyone knew the story now. She really was the black sheep of the family. It was everywhere. Social media never forgets.

At a wedding she attended once, two women were gossiping about her wasting her life.

Maybe one day, she will learn to get over it.

. . ∞ . .

FIVE HOURS LATER, IYAWA got out of her Jeep Wrangler and threw her keys to a guard standing in front of the house.

She took a deep breath, her heels echoing in the silence as she walked on the long pathway widening out to the front entrance of her father's magnificent building, one of the biggest on Kling's Avenue.

The old man quite liked luxury. One could tell by the angel fountains at each corner. The white stucco walls of the mansion loomed five stories high, with many lights enclosed along, casting a distant gleam over its surface.

A silent prayer tugged at her heart as she approached an expansive entryway with double doors. *Please, let Popsi be asleep. I can't deal with him tonight.*

Iyawa didn't know why her father was always worried about her. She was happy with her life. If he hadn't banned her from having her own house, she wouldn't even be here.

Being a Yoruba lady wasn't easy. It was forbidden for a lady to leave her father's house except if she was getting married. To be honest, Iyawa couldn't stand Yoruba culture and their rules. And the thing she hated most was the mockery given to men or women of marriageable age who refused to tie the knot.

Why can't I just do what I want?

When she got inside, an artificial floral fragrance hit her nose. Iyawa sniffed it in. Her sister was so obsessed with the house smelling nice, she had potpourri in every niche of the dwelling.

If anyone thought the exterior of the mansion was deluxe, they needed to get inside. Everything was high-end décor. From the valuable and famous artworks and paintings on the white walls to the arched antique windows and chandeliers, her father showed how rich he was.

Iyawa halted in her steps and threw her gaze to the decorated high-ceiling. Oh, no.

When she got to the sitting room, she found her father seated on the cushioned cream seat. He was a bald, short man with a white beard and icy eyes that showed no emotion.

On the table in front of him was a white envelope, and her curiosity got the better of her.

Why is he sitting here staring into space? This is not good.

She stood frozen in the middle of the room. "Popsi? W... what are you doing here late in the night? You should be asleep by now."

His expression was tight with strain. "What is the time, Iyawa? Just this evening, you walked out on me when I was talking to you, and now, you are just coming back from who knows where."

"What? I—"

"Do not let me repeat myself. What is the time? *Soro Soke!*"

Iyawa glanced at her gold wristwatch. She knew when he spoke in Yoruba, he was very angry. "Three-thirty."

Her father placed his hand underneath his chin like he was trying to think. "Three-thirty. *Nibo lo lo?* I told Jadesola to send texts, but you didn't reply. There was no reason for you to think you can scare us like that."

Iyawa didn't respond. How could he ask about her whereabouts when he was the reason she'd turned off her phone? And why was he acting like he cared?

"Do you know how worried your sister was? Should a responsible lady be out by this time?" His voice was now high. "Couldn't you at least check your phone?"

She rolled her eyes.

"No lady should be out by this time, and definitely not one of the Jaseths."

Her sense of humour took over, and she couldn't help but let out a sharp laugh. "But I am not out. It's three-thirty, and I am home. Home with you."

Her father's frown went deeper. "Would you ever be serious about your life, Iyawa? I told you you needed to straighten out, and I am certain you went out to do nothing of the sort."

"Popsi, you can't just accuse me with no evidence. I did nothing wrong. I didn't party this time. If you are wondering why I am coming home this time, I went out to have dinner. You can try to avoid the truth, but you said things a parent should never say to a child."

Playing those words in her mind again made her feel something born of shame and anger.

It was typical of her father to use words to attack her. She didn't remember when their relationship got like this, but she was sure she had not much memory of him ever speaking to her kindly, the way he did to her younger sister. When she was really little, he'd not really taken an interest, but they'd managed to make few conversations about how she was faring in school and the sort.

But as she grew older, they began arguing about different things. If it wasn't about wearing decent clothes or getting a boyfriend at eighteen, it was always something else. There was a time when she was about to graduate from high school and he locked her in her room because he didn't want her to go to prom. He claimed there were boys ready to devour young girls like her back then.

Releasing a harsh breath, her father reached for the white envelope, rose from his seat, and walked forward with stiff dignity, stopping in front of her.

He handed it to her. "Take these. Gba lowo mi."

"What is this?" Her brows furrowed.

Her father let his glare do the talking.

She sighed and grabbed the envelope. There were newspaper cut-outs of headlines talking about something new. Below was a blurred screenshot of her Instagram Live.

Iyawa inhaled a deep breath, her mouth thinning with displeasure. She recognized the video. It had been a year since the live video of her drunkenly mimicking her father got out. Popsi was mad when he had first saw it. Why was it resurfacing again?

"*Haba!* When will people stop this? It is my life."

"When will they stop? Maybe when you grow up and act like a woman your age should. Look at your sister, for example. Never once have I stressed over Jadesola. You should be thinking of a bright future, a husband, and not all this macho woman you are forming," he said, his voice raw and harsh. "Why did you even make this video? Now, it's out there again. The web never forgets. Everyone still follow your stories, and with new development in the company, this is bad for business."

Iyawa raised her chin, trying hard not to show any emotion. Every day, she dealt with this. Maybe her father didn't know he did this often. Comparing a child to her sister was so wrong. It was like Jadesola was so much better than her.

"I am sorry, Popsi. I can fix this."

"Fix? You can't even help yourself. I am the one helping you out here. Look, if you were still with your mother—"

She released a burst of choked laughter. "Don't bring my mother into this."

Her father exhaled angrily. "I am just a father who is tired of trying to see to it that his daughter grows up. Don't you see I am trying so hard to get you a better future? I shouldn't have let you off for a long time. Now, I think I need to do something."

"Popsi, maybe you should stop trying. I'm tired of making you see I am no longer that lady," she replied in a low, tormented voice.

Tears threatening, she spun around and stormed out of the sitting room. Her father didn't even bother to call after her. So it was anytime they fought. They would pass altercations until one was ready to give up—usually her. She hurtled up the curved stairs to the hallway leading to her room.

When she got there, she slammed the door so hard, the frame on the wall crashed on the marble tiles.

She fell flat on the king-size bed, screaming into the pillow.

Her lungs were constricting, making it hard for her to breathe. She didn't *like* arguing with her father, but no matter how much she tried to show her true self to him, he never understood her. Although Iyawa was plagued by her father's words, there was still a stab of guilt buried in her chest.

Just then, the door opened, and she heard light footsteps. She pinched her lips tight to keep them from trembling.

A weight sank into the bed next to her, and she felt the warmth of a hand caressing her hair.

"Iyawa, Dad is not in his right senses now. He is just mad the video would get in hands of investors coming to the company. You know I love you. I am so sorry."

Swallowing the sob rising in her throat, she looked up at her sister. Jadesola was averagely tall and caramel-skinned, just like their father. Unlike Iyawa, who had brown skin the colour of espresso. Her mother had always compared her skin to Lupita Nyong'o's, but even so, Iyawa couldn't help but notice how different she was from her family members.

Her sister was dressed in blue pyjamas, and with her on the bed was a brown tray containing a plate of apples and a black knife.

"Jadesola," Iyawa croaked.

A tear fell from her eye. Even with their father's excessive comparison between her and her sister, Iyawa loved her deeply. She couldn't bring herself to hate Jadesola, even if she wanted to. She was just seven when Jadesola was born. She'd been the happiest to know she had a baby sister and would draw both of them in her drawing book.

When Jadesola's mother died of cancer two years after giving birth to her, Iyawa made sure she lacked nothing. Jadesola's mother was a very nice woman who treated Iyawa as her child so her death devastated her—and their father, who then had to raise two girls on his own. Well, with the help of nannies.

But while growing up, Iyawa had vowed to be the best sister to Jadesola, and it seemed like Jadesola had made the same vow.

Jadesola shifted the tray on the bed and hugged Iyawa, caressing her back. "I don't know why Popsi keeps doing this. I have to talk to him. This is not cool."

Wiping her tears, she looked at her sister. "No. No. You can't tell him anything, please. It'll only make it worse."

Jadesola frowned. "Iyawa, he treats you badly. I won't take this from him. I don't care about your ego. Something needs to be done."

"No, Jadesola. Please, just let him be."

"He talks about what you *do*, yet he doesn't know you. Who fought for me back in high school when everyone laughed at me for my braces?" Jadesola sighed. "Who was there for me, all those nights I cried about my mother being dead? It was all you."

Iyawa gave a small smile. "Hey, you looked good with braces. Those boys were spewing nonsense."

"Everyone knew my braces phase made me look horrible." Jadesola cupped Iyawa's cheeks with her hands. "Please, cheer up. You know I don't like seeing you sad."

"Did you bring these apples for me? How did you know I have not taken anything?"

Jadesola chuckled. "You don't really eat when you go out to bars. And besides, I didn't hear you replying Popsi as you used to so I figured you were hungry."

"Ah, you know me better than anyone else." Iyawa grabbed one of the apples and took a bite. "Thanks for this."

For a moment, silence enveloped the room. It suddenly seemed like her big room wasn't so big again. She knew the next words her sister was going to say.

Iyawa chewed slowly. "Jadesola, don't ask me that."

Jadesola raised her hand in surrender. "But I am curious. You know I support anything you do, but I just want to know why you go live every time you get drunk."

Iyawa gave her a look. "I also don't know. At least, you guys have nothing to worry about. I haven't partied in months now."

"I thank God for you, though."

Thank you, Sis. I wish Popsi can just see this new me and not effects of the past."

"He will. Just give him time."

Iyawa sank back into the bed and reached for another apple. It was like with every apple, her hunger was increasing.

It was times like this she was most grateful for her sister. Sometimes, Jadesola didn't understand her, but at least, she showed Iyawa she was willing to try.

Chapter Two

Iyawa groaned. She observed the traffic through her window. Was she ever going to make it in time for the meeting?

It had been an hour since she got stuck in this Ikeja jam, but the cars and buses on three different queues didn't seem to show any hope of moving forward. She had to get work in time to submit this document she had just received. Those papers meant that the Nigerian basketball team would use the TeleInc logo on their team kits for three years. Although Lagos was one of the most amusing cities in Nigeria, the traffic issue made it a very stressful one. It was just so crowdy.

She observed it all through her window. Alongside the road sat a canteen with heaps of filth in front waiting to be cleared. Hawkers were walking in between the traffic selling bottled water and Gala for passengers. Situations like this made them sell very well.

"Buy your pure water and bottle water. Pure water, ten-ten naira." A middle-aged woman in a shirt and Ankara wrapper around her waist walked between the vehicles.

There were people walking through the cars, crossing the road to the other side. *Okadas,* also known as motorcycle taxis, could be seen riding along the small spaces between cars. If there was anything about Okadas in Nigeria, they were very impatient, unlike the *Keke Maruwas,* popularly known as tricycle.

Iyawa was so hot, she had to wind down the window of her car, exposing her to the stares of the passengers in the yellow buses next to her. Some people on the bus were fanning themselves with paper, some pointlessly using their hands. Some had slept off, sweat dripping from their heads.

How can one sleep in a condition this?

Iyawa sighed. Typical Nigerians.

Soon, the cars began moving at low speed, and Iyawa ignited the engine of her car. But as she was about to move forward, a small white car with vegetables and sacks peeking at the booth, which had been decorated with ropes, attempted to cut into her lane.

This left a frown on her face. No, no. She was already late.

Iyawa urged her car forward, colliding with the other vehicle. The impact wasn't huge, but it made the driver angry.

He stopped his engine, leaning forward to face her.

"Shey ya were ni?" The passengers in his car were also pinning her with the death glare.

He was cutting into a lane, and he still had the guts to ask her if she was mad.

She hit her steering wheel in annoyance. *What is wrong with this driver?* The other drivers were now honking for him to move forward and forget arguing with her.

"Ikan te shey yen, sho da? Na all of us dis traffic go affect," she told him.

"Aunty, you no suppose hit im car. shey na because you get big car?" one of his passengers, a female seated in the front seat, replied her.

She was about giving a reply when her phone rang. Arghh! She was going to have to let this man win the argument.

She wound up her window, the man taking up a space in front of her. She inched her car forward as the cars on the queue moved slowly.

Her phone rang again. It was in her bag, yet it sounded like it rang next to her ears.

Who is calling me now?

She stretched to the passenger seat and reached for her bag. Her father was going to be so angry.

The manager for the Nigerian basketball team, Alaba—one of the most important personalities in Lekki city—had also delayed her. Lekki was a city in Lagos known for its beaches and beautiful estates. His office was a two-hour journey from theirs, but he wasted her time in signing the documents. She had managed to pass through the small traffic at Lekki toll-gate but was now stuck in Ikeja's.

When she got hold of her phone, she picked up the call with a sigh.

"Im. Thank goodness you finally picked."

She could hear the relief in her sister's voice.

"Hey, Jadesola. What's up?"

"Dad is up. We have been waiting for you at the office. It's eight minutes to twelve already. You have been gone since six in the morning," Jadesola said, rushing over words.

"Jadesola, haven't you heard of traffic? I'm on my way. This traffic is not moving at all."

She heard Jadesola's sigh of frustration. "Great, I thought you leaving early will avoid traffic."

Iyawa placed a hand on her face. "Same here. Old Alaba delayed me, too. Man was just talking about his achievements of having a great team. I mean, I hate football."

"Ah, but we won the bid to sponsor the team, right?" Jadesola chuckled. "That will make up for it."

"Yeah. Whatever." She could sense Jadesola's hesitation. "What is it this time?"

"There is someone here that I know will get to your blood. I don't know why the person is here, but promise me you won't freak out."

Iyawa narrowed her eyes. "Who?"

A high-pitched laughter resulted from the other end. "Someone."

"Sis, tell me—"

"Sorry, I can't hear you. Bye," her sister said in a sing-song tone.

Iyawa leaned her head back on the seat, trying to suppress a sigh. *I just want to go home and sleep.*

Fortunately for her, vehicles began moving at a faster rate. She ignited the engine and moved.

When she parked her car in front of her favourite coffee shop to get a coffee—just two blocks from her father's company—what she didn't expect was to collide with a woman carrying a tray of coffee at the entrance.

"Ah!" She stepped back, trying to dab off the brown stain on her suit. She had been wearing a turquoise, long-sleeve vintage design blazer and pencil suit sure to compliment her looks.

"I am so sorry. I was rushing. I didn't mean to," the lady said, stretching forth a napkin to Iyawa.

Iyawa tugged at her clothing. It was like her skin was burning.

The fair-skinned lady really seemed genuine with her apology. Her brows were tugged in an agonizing expression. "I was going to deliver this to my boss and his friends. I was rushing. He is going to kill me."

Iyawa mustered a smile and collected the napkin. "It's okay. I am fine. Do you have money to buy another cup of that coffee?"

The woman shook her head.

Iyawa dipped her hand into her pocket and gave her a one-thousand naira note. "Take it. Get your boss another cup."

The lady's face spread into a big smile. "Oh, thank you. Thank you."

Luckily for her, there was a big boutique blocks away from the company. She made a mental note to stop there and get new clothes.

When she had gotten to the boutique and had chosen a new red gown ending above her knees to fit with her black ankle boots, she headed for the checkout counter.

When she got in front of the cashier and issued her card, her mounting fear increased as she watched the male cashier swipe her card several times.

Oh, no. No. Please, don't let it be what I'm thinking. Iyawa chewed on her lips in silence, dreading her greatest fear.

"Ma'am, it seems your card is blocked from making transactions," the hairy man said to her.

She looked at the gown and shoes on the counter and turned back to the man. "Can you please try it again? It could be an error."

The cashier did as he was told. "Same thing, ma'am. I am sorry."

Iyawa let out an irritable sigh as she collected her card. That old man had beaten her faster than she expected. Now, she was going to show up there stained with coffee and be double-embarrassed.

Today wasn't going exactly as well for her as she'd planned. She hated Lagos traffic. They always made a mess of people. Iyawa was still contemplating her next actions when a hand stretched forth from behind with a blue card.

"Never mind. Add her expenses to mine. I'm buying a tie," a delicate, smooth yet familiar voice said behind her, dropping a new blue tie on the counter.

No. She had to reject it. No man should ever spend on her. They would hold on to it and expect something in return, and she had nothing to offer.

Men and their mentality.

As she swivelled to meet the gaze of the man nice enough to help her, she came face to chin with the one person she'd thought she'd never see again.

Oh. Today is a bad day. It has been confirmed.

"You! Matthias," she mumbled, gritting her teeth. "What in the world are you doing here?"

Matthias smirked. "Ah, my dear. Nice to see you."

He still looked the same. He was tall, beardless, with an appealing face.

Eight years ago, she'd had a crush on him. Now, she wasn't even sure.

Why does he always seem to have an effect on me?

What was he even doing here?

The cashier collected the card and was about to swipe it when Iyawa stopped him.

"No. I can't pay for the gown and shoes, and I am extremely okay with that. I don't need pity cash."

Matthias waved her off. "Please go on with what you are doing. She doesn't have cash, so let her be."

Iyawa bit on her lip in anger. Her body temperature had already increased. She hadn't really thought of how she would react if she saw him again. He was the son of her father's friend. Someone she didn't know existed until eight years ago. Being a businessman, her father had so many friends, but Matthias was just someone she couldn't forget.

Everyone knew the Bades—they were just as popular as the Jaseth family, but they could never beat the Jaseth to fame. The Bades owned a smart mobile accessories band called BDS in Ikeja. Iyawa believed TeleInc was more famous. Her father's company had sponsored many events, sport teams, and even Nollywood TV shows where their commercials could be seen. TeleInc was better.

She gave him a cold stare. It happened Matthias was once the guy her father had wanted her to date, but he'd rejected her, saying her lifestyle was too weird for him.

He'd even had the guts to say he didn't want to be dumped anytime soon.

Naturally, Iyawa would never accept favours from Matthias Bade, but it seemed she had no choice. Unless she wanted to make her already mad father go insane by wearing such a stained suit, she needed to accept this.

"I am going to take your offer because I didn't ask for it." She pinned on a half-smile.

Matthias chuckled. "Of course you didn't. You would never."

When the cashier stretched forth a shopping bag with her clothes, Iyawa collected it with a huff and stormed off to the dressing room as directed by a worker.

When she came out looking all neat with her hair let down, she didn't expect to still find Matthias waiting.

She groaned. "Don't you have anything else to do?"

Matthias shrugged as he took in her outfit. "My presence bothers you? Last time I checked, this boutique is for everyone."

"Wait, don't tell me my father sent you again. That is so stupid of you."

Matthias paused, his gaze running over her face again. It was like he was trying to say something.

She feigned surprise. "Ew, are you jobless? Stop staring at me like that."

"Well, well, well. What a sight." His eyes grew wide with amusement. "You still look the same."

If she wasn't hating on him right now, she would have taken a moment to admire his handsome features. He was dressed in a grey tuxedo that made him look like some hectic bodyguard. His short-textured haircut brought out the beauty of his golden-brown face, making him seem like a man every woman needed. He just stood there looking devilishly gorgeous.

"Please, tell me you weren't sent by my dad to spy on me," she repeated, walking past him.

He followed her out of the shop. "As much as the thought would excite you, I'm sorry to say everything isn't about you, baby girl. I came here to get a new tie."

She stopped in front of her car, making sure her look told him she didn't believe a word he said. "Do not call me baby girl.

A new tie? This is what you came up with. Matthias, did my father invite you or not?"

He dipped his hands into his pockets and nodded. "Yes. I don't know why, but I think my father knows about this meeting. Maybe it's about a new collaboration or something. Why are you even asking?"

"I just wanted to know why. Jadesola called me, and it kind of sounded urgent. It was like she thought I wasn't going to be happy."

Iyawa's face widened with realization. Matthias was the guy Jadesola said was going to make her blood boil.

Matthias chuckled. "Maybe you did something wrong again. I know that face. The mischievous look."

"I love living up to your expectations, but I don't think I have done anything yet to get Popsi angry." She gave him a cocky smile.

Matthias crossed his arms, a smile finding its way up to his lips. "Iyawa Jaseth, I don't believe you."

"Well, I don't want you to." She assessed his face. "I just want to know why my father invited you. I don't like saying this, but I fear my father's impromptu meetings. That man is not to be trusted."

"Enough talking. Let's go if you want to find out. You and I can catch up later. I don't think you want to keep your father waiting." Matthias yanked open the front passenger seat and hopped in.

She blinked, then gave him a lifeless stare. "Okay, out of my Jeep, Matthias. Off you go."

"What? You don't expect me to walk back to the office. I didn't bring my car along."

She shrugged. "Why didn't you bring your car? If you walked here, you can walk back. It is so funny that you even think I care."

He grabbed the seat belt, giving her a wink. "I didn't want to stress myself. The boutique isn't far from the office, but now you're here, you can give me a lift. Be a gentle lady."

She clenched her hands around the steering wheel as she drove away from the boutique. This was what she hated about him. Him teasing her every time like she was some teenager. He was just thirty-two, yet he treated a thirty-year-old lady as a child.

"How about that girlfriend of yours? Getting married soon?"

Matthias shook his head. "I'm not going to talk about my life. Not with you."

"You avoided the girlfriend part," she pointed. "Something must have happened."

"We aren't together anymore. No more questions."

She breathed out. Of course, no more questions.

It didn't take long for her to arrive at the company. Stepping out of her car, she dipped her hand into her bag and dropped her keys. She stood in front of her father's glass building structure with TeleInc written beside a big star logo, the one plastered on all of their gadgets.

She couldn't help but admire the way it exuded magnificence. TeleInc headquarters stood in the middle of tall buildings that also belonged to the company, so different, but each reflecting the beauty of the Ikeja GRA. Flowers of different colours covered the edges of the building. Located in Ikeja, it was the most ever-bubbling place she had seen. Well-paved roads, traffic lights, and regular power supply—no one could resist this place.

She could feel Matthias standing beside her.

"Don't tell me you are terrified. I think your father was in a good mood," Matthias said.

Iyawa bit down hard on her lip. "Do I look scared? I am ready for him."

"Is there a day you never get ready?"

As they entered the building, it was a display of employees walking with files in their hands, some in duos. Large screens were up, showing the ads for TeleInc phones and laptop with the voice-over of a female. Celebrities and athletes could be seen on the screen endorsing their gadgets.

She responded to their greetings as she made her way to the elevator. Neither Iyawa nor Matthias said a word to one another while in the carriage. She could feel his gaze burning a hole through her neck.

When the bell dinged, the doors opened to reveal Jadesola and her father's secretary waiting in front of her father's office. The hall was filled with so many plants and flowers, one would think it was a garden. Her family had an obsession with plants and gardens and herbs.

On the wall was a picture frame of her father with a name tag at the bottom. He was smiling so hard, you'd think he smiled so often.

A playful grin spread on her sister's lips. "Where have you been? The traffic caused this much delay?"

"Busy having fun and fetching the documents, of course." She handed the folder to her sister. "I have a lot to tell you about my terrible morning, but first, where is the old man?"

"Popsi will be out here any minute." Jadesola turned to look at Matthias, her gaze travelling to his new tie. "Oh, you have gotten a new tie, and you've met Iyawa."

Matthias brushed his tie in a dramatic manner.

"Your father wonders why you delay so much," Jadesola added.

"Oh, I met up with dear Iyawa here. We did have a lot to catch up on. Did you know she couldn't buy things with her card anymore? That is a shocker."

She could kill this guy. "Shut your mouth, Matthias, before I shut it for you."

Jadesola exclaimed in annoyance. "Im, is that true? Did he block your account?"

Before Iyawa could assure her sister all was well, her father came out of the office. Beside him was Matthias's father and two bodyguards dressed in suits. The expression on their faces didn't sit well with Iyawa.

"Iyawa Jaseth, what took you so long?" her father said, his voice a little too low for her liking.

"Good morning to you, too, Popsi." She gave a mischievous smile.

Jadesola nudged her arm. "Popsi, Iyawa brought the documents. It was really stressful with all the traffic and all, but she got it signed."

Her father's expression softened a bit. "Oh. Traffic in Ikeja is something I don't like. Sorry about that."

She felt a strange sense of comfort as she turned to Matthias's father. "Good afternoon, Mr Bade. How are you?"

"Good morning, Miss Iyawa," Matthias's father greeted from his place beside her father. "I am doing so well, thank you."

Unlike her short father, Mr Bade was tall, and she saw a slight resemblance between Matthias and his father.

"Do you know why I've called you and Matthias today?" her father asked.

Iyawa frowned. She passed a curious gaze to Matthias, only to have it returned.

"Me and Matthias? I thought this meeting was business."

Her father shook his head. "It isn't about business. Something more personal."

She crossed her arms and looked away. She didn't have any energy to argue.

As if she could read her mind, Jadesola held her shoulder. "Im, calm down. Let him speak."

"Iyawa, my dear. It's just that your father called me down here about some issues, and after a long talk, we think this decision is the best," Mr Bade said.

"What did my father tell you?" Her reply held a bit of impatience.

"That you and Matthias are going to be engaged to one another."

For a moment, silence covered the room with its cloak, and it was possible to hear everyone breathing so hard.

And as if it was going to help, her father added, "Fake engagement, of course."

"Excuse me. I mean you. You can't just call me here and drop something like this. How does this relate to business?" Matthias asked, his eyes showing a wash of disbelief.

"We've had the meeting, Jaseth and I. The outcome is that we get you two engaged," Mr Bade said.

Surely, she must have heard wrong or this was a joke. There was no way she could have heard this right. Get engaged to Matthias? For what?

"Father. What are you saying? You should have spoken to me first."

"You two are getting engaged, Matthias," Mr Bade said. "I thought you two were cool friends."

"What? Your son and I aren't friends. Where did you even get the idea from? I can't even stand him."

"I agree with her on this one. I don't like some things about her." Matthias glared at her.

Iyawa raised her hands in exasperation. "I need to be excused. This place is giving me vibes I don't like."

"There is nothing to be excused about. No one here speaks Swahili. Everything is self-explanatory."

Her father's unconcerned demeanour continued to irk her.

"You all might as well start speaking Swahili. I am not getting engaged to anyone. Not today nor ever! You can't make decisions without telling me. This is delusional," she yelled.

This was baffling. How did she get from a horrible morning to a fiancée in one day?

"I always tell you to watch your tone when speaking to me." Her father flayed her with his gaze.

"Popsi, I told you, stop controlling Iyawa. It is not nice." Jadesola frowned.

Her father pointed at her sister. "You stay out of it."

A sudden coldness hit her at the core. "Bu...but why? I didn't do anything wrong."

"Our reaction is perfectly normal. You didn't tell us about this. Father, you could have informed me first," Matthias said. His voice was filled with anger and a hint of hurt.

Mr Bade sighed. "Matthias, dear, it had to be done. You should understand better."

Matthias wrinkled his face. "Father, she is Iyawa. Do you know what that means? How can you agree to this?"

"And he is whiny. Like a puppy. I mean, who believes in true love and all that?" She threw her hands up.

"Hey, I believe in true love," Jadesola says.

"I am not getting engaged to anyone, Popsi. Fake or not. This is crazy. You can't just force me into a relationship for no reason." She gave her father a glassy stare.

"This is because of you. You are just too naïve to realize the damage you are causing upon your life, and now, it is affecting my business," her father said.

"Popsi. If there is a reason why you are doing this, tell us," Jadesola let out, placing a reassuring hand on Iyawa's shoulder.

She watched as her father's demeanour relaxed. He snapped his fingers at the bodyguard next to him, and an envelope was handed over to him. He gave it to Jadesola.

"Bade and I have been working on a collaboration, and we are launching one of our best gadgets soon. We expect investors to be there that day, but with the news keeping tabs on your sister's life, she is going to spoil our business if I don't do something."

"Popsi—

"No, Jadesola. You can't help her this time. Bade is a good friend of mine, and Matthias is a nice guy. We just need her to look good and settled 'til the event is over. This engagement will calm everything down. TeleSpark 10 is coming out in three months, and I can't risk it. So, for the next three months, she will use this engagement to clean her dirt. I can't deal with all these scandals."

Iyawa could feel her veins twitching as her eyes caught the headlines. *"Iyawa Jaseth, daughter of famous James Jaseth – We've heard of cases of spoilt, entitled party kids, but with women? Iyawa is about to break records."*

How was she going to spend three months with someone she hated?

She sniffed back the tears and glanced at her father. Could faking an engagement with Matthias earn her back her respect and dignity? But she didn't even like Matthias.

"So now, I am the one that gets stuck with her, huh?" Matthias hissed.

She lowered her gaze. "I...I don't know what to say. C...can't it be with someone else?"

Her father's stance was unaltered. "My decision remains the same. We will pick a date where you two will pretend to be having a dinner and a public proposal."

"Don't I get to decide what I want? It's like no one is listening," Matthias insisted.

Iyawa met his gaze for a while. She tried to read his expression but couldn't pick out any definition. Oh, she was embarrassed. All her dirty linen washed in front of him. Again.

Matthias frowned at his father. "I can't believe I got a new tie for this."

"Relax, Matthias. Her reputation is destroyed. If she is going to be the next CEO of this company, people have to take her seriously. They have to treat her with respect. She has to lay low," her father explained.

"And I am the only man in this world to help her?" Matthias asked. "I am sure she has men to help her."

Mr Bade puffed out. "You are the perfect fake-fiancé. Besides, after the launching event, you can both break up if you want to."

Iyawa shifted uneasily. This conversation was so uncomfortable. "You couldn't even come up with someone I can cope with? We are going to kill ourselves, and that is on all of you."

Matthias' lips thinned in anger. "And what if it doesn't work? How are we so sure she would even stop?"

"I didn't say I was going to agree to this." She gave him a glassy stare.

"I can't believe you can still be cocky during a situation like this. It seems like you need my help."

She searched for a better reply, but she knew Matthias was right. If she wanted to be the next CEO, she had to give in to her father's ridiculous plan.

Iyawa gave a shallow breath. "Let's say we agree to this. What are the things we have to do?"

A devilish smile spread out on her father's face. "You guys will have to go out on dates, be seen together a lot, and act like you are madly in love. That's all."

Colour drained from her face. "What?"

"We need to get this scandal erased from our name," her father replied.

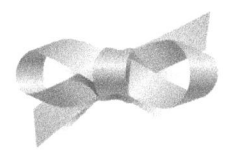

Chapter Three

Iyawa gave a hard swallow as she turned away from the mirror.

Her sister inspected her outfit with a pleased expression. "Oh, I love it. It is beautiful. Don't you love it?"

Iyawa wrinkled her nose. Yes, the gown was beautiful—an above-the-knee blue flare gown with flower petals embroidered all around it.

"I don't care about the gown, Jadesola. I care about what is going to happen to me."

Jadesola slumped on Iyawa's bed, looking at her with a smile. "Relax. It is just dinner."

"Dinner with Matthias! I don't like the guy." Her jaw was starting to cause discomfort from all the tightness.

"I hope you realize you are going to have lots of dinners and outings with him. You might even meet his family. Babe, get ready."

"I am doomed." She felt the painful lump in her throat. How was she going to cope with Matthias? Today was the day of the proposal, and she wasn't even excited one bit.

Jadesola sighed. "Look, I don't know if this is going to work, but if you look from Dad's perspective, it is worth a try."

She folded her arms. "What do you mean? Me getting engaged wouldn't make people like me and respect me. It is absurd."

"Yes, it will."

"No one thinks this way."

"I want you to imagine you are a wealthy woman who wants to invest in a company."

Iyawa gave a snort. "I am not doing this with you. I have so much going on right now."

"Humour me, please."

She rolled her eyes. "Fine, I am imagining."

"But there are two famous companies. One is owned by a married lady with good reputation, and the other is owned by a woman who is known for, you know... Which will you choose?" Jadesola asked, darting a curious gaze at her.

Iyawa's shoulders sagged. *It was a big question.*

Jadesola sat up on the bed and flayed her sister with her gaze. "Would you choose the latter?"

"Would you even agree to this ridiculous plan if it was you?" Iyawa fixed her with a stare.

"Yes! If I caused such scandals that could be an obstacle to my dreams, I would do anything. This isn't only about Dad. It's about image and reputation. Do you know how bad I feel when ladies at these functions say my sister will never be able to get a husband because she is loose?"

Iyawa blew out a breath. "My life shouldn't be an issue to you all. If I don't care about my past, you shouldn't. God will get me my own man. If Popsi is so tired of me, why doesn't he talk about my mother? I could go live with her or something."

Jadesola's eyebrows pulled together. "Iyawa, you know I love you, but I can't provide answers. Don't you want to be happy, Iyawa? Why don't you just try this for yourself and the company, and if it doesn't work out, we can always come up with something else."

The company. The company. That was all they cared about. Nobody was going to help her now. She was doing this.

. . ⚜ . .

SHE HAULED THE STEERING wheel to the left and finally parked near a big, exquisite building with a tag reading WAZOBIA RESTAURANT. When she got down from her car, she observed the place. It had a sense of serenity around its creamy walls with a balmy exterior. She couldn't help but compliment Matthias's taste. Although he lived on the other side of Ikeja, he had managed to choose a restaurant that wouldn't inconvenience both sides.

Sashaying her way in, she paused when she was greeted warmly by a staff at the door. The restaurant was high-toned with its low lights and simple colour scheme providing a romantic atmosphere. Fresh flowers abounded, with golden chandeliers and candle light illuminating its beauty. Even the slow music being played sent her into a lighter mood.

She glanced around the restaurant. People were seated in twos around a table, and she wondered how she was going to find him in such a big space.

A waiter dressed in white suit walked up to her. "Welcome to Wazobia Restaurant. Take a seat, ma'am, and I will send someone to get your orders."

She smiled gently. "Sorry, I am looking for someone. If I could just look around and find him."

"Did he leave a reservation? Should we check?" the waiter asked.

How was she supposed to know all this? All he did was send an address of the restaurant asking her to make it in time.

"The guy is dumb. I don't know if he did, but if I can just call him, we will find out," she said, reaching for her phone in her bag.

Her gaze finally caught hold of Matthias sitting in a corner, looking clearly distracted. *His profile is so intimidating.* He was wearing a blue suit, peering down at his phone as he pressed on.

"Ah, that's him. I will go now. Thank you."

After walking between tables, she finally reached him and coughed to earn his attention.

"How can you be so relaxed? This isn't your bedroom."

Matthias looked up, easing into a smile. "Hello, look who finally came. I almost thought you were kidnapped or something."

"This is so strange. Yesterday, you hated me for this. Why are you smiling now?"

She found it almost impossible to return his smile. *Why is he looking so attractive?*

"I realized I like doing favours. Especially to those in dire need of it. No need to thank me." He was now grinning.

She took a seat in front of him. "I don't need your help, you know that."

"Then why are you here?"

"My father thinks I need your help. I almost bailed out on this stupid dinner, but thanks to my little sister, I'm here."

Matthias paused, his gaze caressing her body. "I like your gown. Coincidentally, I'm also wearing blue."

"And I hate your face." Her body grew hot.

He reached for his glass of water and took a sip. "I know. I like your eyes, though. They look pretty."

A shiver ran through her body. What was this? Was he pulling her leg?

"Stop flirting with me. Not in a situation like this."

"What? You've been telling me you hate me for a long time now. Say something new. I'm trying my best here." He winked at her.

"That is not the key thing here. Let's order a drink and talk about nothing so we can waste time before we pull off this proposal drama." She took a quick glance around the room. "That is if these people believe our ruse."

"Relax. All you have to do is smile and act like you are in love with me. It is quite simple. People in love do smile a lot," Matthias said.

"Act like I am in love with you? Have you seen you? I can't even think about your face without feeling nauseous."

Matthias's mouth quirked up in amusement. "You say you hate me, but sometimes, I find it hard to believe you. You don't even act like you hate me."

"How do I act, then?"

"Like you love being around someone like me."

Her ears were now going red. She hated when someone implied she couldn't be truthful. He was an attractive young man. She knew a good thing when she saw it, but she just didn't want this good thing.

Iyawa ignored him and called a waiter as they ordered a bottle of wine and dinner.

When their orders came in and they began digging in, and once they were done eating in silence, Matthias leaned in his seat as he watched her.

"So?"

Iyawa's nose wrinkled. "So what?"

"How do we do this? Do I propose now? Is this the right time?" he whispered.

"If I didn't know better, I would say you are much more excited about this. I'm not even worried. Do you have anywhere you need to be tonight?"

He looked at her critically. "Why do you care?"

"I don't. I was just asking."

"No, I don't have anywhere to be tonight."

He dipped his hand into his suit and brought out a velvet ring box. Iyawa searched for an explanation for his calmness. Something was wrong with his reaction to getting engaged to her, and she was going to find out.

"Don't tell me you bought a ring for this," she said. "I hope you realize this is fake, right?"

Matthias snickered. "Please, you think I would want this for myself? My father got this for me."

He was right. Why would he be so excited about getting engaged to someone he didn't stand?

"Fine. Just do it so we can leave."

He blinked. "God, please smile. You are about to get a proposal, so be happy."

"I will try to act like this isn't one of my biggest nightmares." She gave him a wicked smile.

Matthias stood up from his chair, dropping on one knee as he opened the velvet box. This time, everyone in the restaurant was looking in their direction. Some women had their hands over their mouth in sweet adoration while some men watched with a smile. Some people were staring with curiosity while some, including some waitress, had their phones flipped out from their pocket.

"Stop smiling for now. Act like you weren't expecting it, will you?" Matthias muttered.

Iyawa tried not to laugh. "Oh, you look stupid. So stupid, I wish I took a picture of this."

"Eight years ago, when we first met during that business meeting, I thought you were hot. You had this aura of confidence around you that astonished me. Right there in that board room, my heart was peeking at the gorgeous lady sitting in front of me."

The restaurant was rocked with soft chuckles and Awws.

Oh, God.

Matthias's voice was soft, and the way his eyes sparkled, it...it felt so real, but she knew better. She couldn't help but stare at him. When they first met, their introduction had been short, and he didn't even for once look at her during that boardroom meeting. She knew this because she had been sneaking glances at him.

She managed a smile, putting her hand to her chest in fake surprise. She had watched so many romance movies not to know how this went.

Matthias licked his lips as he continued. "It wasn't until I walked up to you and asked you out for lunch that I knew I couldn't stop thinking about you. What do you say? I do, do you?"

There was something seductive in his look, and it wasn't until her eyes caught sight of his lips that she realized what it was. There was a tingling sensation in her gut as thoughts not entirely appropriate right now flashed through her mind.

"Say yes! Say yes!"

A hint of annoyance rested in Matthias's gaze.

She swallowed. "Yes, I do. I do."

Matthias slid the diamond ring down her finger. It fitted perfectly. *How did his father even know my size?*

People stood up clapping as he rose from his seat and placed a subtle kiss on her cheek. For a moment, her thoughts rushed to that spot. What was wrong with her?

After making sure people had taken pictures and thanking everyone for their wonderful congratulations, Matthias held her hand as they walked out of the restaurant. The breeze was strong, blowing her hair across her face.

"Wow. That went well," he said.

Iyawa stood in front of her car. "I hope my father is happy when he sees those pictures online. I can't believe he wants us to live together."

Matthias dipped his hands into his pockets as he leaned on her car. "Yes, about that. I don't really like the idea, too. Is it really necessary?"

She sighed. "According to our fathers, it is. He wants me to be at your place this weekend for another outing. Quick question, do you live with your parents?"

"Jeez, I'm a grown man. No, I have my own house. What do you even think of me?" he asked with a puzzled frown.

"It was just a question."

He leaned closer. "This is where we say goodbye? It was nice, though."

She melted in the comfort of his nearness. "What was nice?"

"This dinner. It might not occur to you, but we just went on our first date."

"Good night, Matthias."

He held her hand, licking his lips once again. What was it with him and his lips?

"You can't just leave."

She tilted her head to the other side. "Is there something else?"

"We are engaged now. Let it sink. No playing around."

"Goodbye, Matthias."

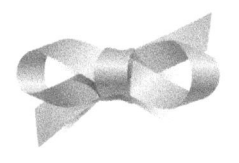

Chapter Four

It'd been three days since the proposal, and her phone had been lighting up with tags and notifications. Social media was bustling with news and pictures about her fake engagement to Matthias. People were nice with words, congratulating them while others were feeling pity for Matthias.

Now driving to his office, Iyawa couldn't help but feel tired. How long was she going to make people see them together?

When the car stopped at a beautiful cream-colored two-story building, the first detail to catch her eye were the larger-than-life floor-to-ceiling windows, which gave the room a pretty look when she reached it.

Matthias's luxury office was so big and airy, with ceramics on display and house plants.

The thing about his office was that he used muted tones and serious colours like her house. His was a play of colour palettes with some balance of complimenting prints.

Hmm, not bad.

She sat on the brown, plush sofa placed beside a large ottoman accented with fluffy cushions and a throw. It was then Matthias walked into the room, looking all sweaty. He was dressed in a tie-and-dye joggers and sweat shirt combo, with ear pods and a bottle of water.

He paused to catch his breath. "I didn't know you were going to come this early, Iyawa. It is just seven in the morning. What do you want?"

"Why do you like to complain about everything I do?" she asked with a frown. "My father asked me to come here so we could go out after."

"I was not complaining. I was just telling you I didn't get to finish my jogging session." He sat on the couch next to her.

Before he could reply, his ringing phone interrupted her.

"Do you mind if I take this call? It is kind of important."

She groaned, waving him off.

And with that, he walked out of the room.

Iyawa studied her surroundings with scrutiny. She'd never thought she would pray to be back in her father's house.

Matthias shook his head again as he returned to her, a heavy sigh coming from his mouth. "If I was told yesterday that I was going to be someone's fiancé, I would have laughed it off. Now add the fact I was going to be *your* fiancé, I would have made a bet on all my money."

She raised an eyebrow. "Do I look happy? Look at you. You seemed pretty relaxed and ready to go through all this on the night you proposed."

"Fake-proposed," he corrected. "I got to know about it that day at the office. Look at me, you can guess I would have loved to get properly engaged. I was brought up by a Christian mother."

She snorted. "Trust you? I am not doing that! You don't even know me, yet you silently agreed."

"You think I knew about this earlier? No. Trust me, I didn't know."

"Trust you?" She scoffed. "I don't think so."

"Iyawa. I am saying the truth. I am not lying."

"Then why did you agree to the engagement? Why does your father agree? I mean, what really do you gain out of this?"

"My father."

She raised an eyebrow.

"Look, he had problems with his company. This partnership is his only chance."

"What?" She squinted.

"He told me the night after we left the office," Matthias added. "I also didn't know."

"Your father kind of sold you for money?"

He scowled. "My father is not like that. He had no other options. And as his son, my only duty is to help him when he needs my help. And besides, your father came up with this. Fake an engagement to remove you from the spotlight, and he helps us. Thinking about it now, I don't think it is a big deal."

Anger boiled inside her. She couldn't believe her father could trick his friend into something like this. Because of him, she was stuck. Matthias himself was no saint. He was only doing this because of money.

She gritted her teeth. "That father of mine. Always acting like he owns the world."

"I know you are angry, but this man cares for you. I can sense it."

"Yes. Of course. You would say nice things now after the things he promised your dad." She scoffed.

Matthias shifted uncomfortably in his seat. "Don't talk like that. You are making my father sound bad somehow for agreeing to this. The man is going through a lot."

"It is not about your father. You are a hypocrite. No, I can't get engaged to Iyawa. No, I am not the right man for her. A benefit comes in, and you want to be the hero now. It doesn't work like that."

The expressions he'd made that day at the office came rushing in. He wasn't happy, and now, he was cool because he had an advantage.

"I'm—"

She raised her hand to stop him. "I'm going to make your life miserable. Trust me."

"That is if you don't fall in love with me." He was now smiling.

The colour drained from her face. "Fall in love with you? Who do you think you are? The best of the best? I can't even stand you."

"You can make my life miserable all you want, but I promise you, it won't hurt me."

"I see why your ex left you."

Matthias crossed his arms and watched her with a smirk. "Is that supposed to hurt me or something?"

Iyawa's mouth slackened. "This conversation is over."

Matthias slinked back into his chair. "I didn't know you hated me so much."

"Flash news, I do. In fact, I am already thinking of ways to frustrate you. You think I am going to act as your good fiancée? Impossible." She gave a chuckle.

Matthias leaned closer. "I want to see you try, and I repeat, that is if you don't fall for me."

She stared deep into his eyes and could see determination. Why was he suddenly enjoying this? Maybe he didn't know, but she wasn't a fan of love.

"What if you fall in love with me first? Guys fall in love faster than ladies."

Matthias chuckled. "That is not possible. I cannot love you."

"I am unlovable?"

"I did not say that."

"You meant it."

"You can seriously put words in my mouth."

Iyawa folded her arms. "You are just scared you will fall in love first."

Matthias sighed. "Fine. Challenge on. I assure you these three months will be the months you fall for me! Three months to see if you are able to make me fall in love with you or if I am able to charm my way into that heart of yours. Whoever wins gets to do whatever the other wants."

"That is so ridiculous. I am not doing this." She snorted.

"Are you pulling out because you don't trust your heart? Surely, you know you won't be able to get me to love you."

Reminder: Men are so full of themselves. She hated the fact he thought she could ever fall in love with him. All those years ago, she was attracted to him, and he... well, he wasn't. Now if he wanted to play games, she was ready.

"If you put it like that, I am in. Can I tell you something?" She was now grinning.

"Yes?"

"I still stand by my word. I'm going to frustrate you."

Matthias cocked his head. "The challenge was to make one fall for one. How is that—"

"Believe me when I say even at this, you are going to fail badly. You will love me so much, you will think of me killing a cute puppy, the cutest puppy ever, and you will find it adorable."

Matthias's face grew pale. "I was short of words, and that is strange. I always know what to say."

"You are pathetic for a fiancé, you know. A stupid romantic. Watch me charm you just by being me." She smirked.

"You can call me that. Lest I forget, we have a family dinner at my father's place tomorrow night. So please get dressed in one of your loveliest outfits as I am going to introduce you to everyone as my fiancée."

"Family dinner?" she asked. "People still do that?"

"What? You don't have dinner with your family?"

She shrugged. "Only if me and Popsi make it through without arguing. I mostly eat in my room."

Matthias seemed like he wanted to comment on that but refrained. "My father thinks it's important to let everyone know we are now engaged. To make it more realistic. I guess your scandalous news will change into something gossipier for the press. You are engaged now."

"We are going to have so much fun together, hubby to-be."

Chapter Five

Iyawa walked through the streets, trying to finding the perfect boutique to choose her dress for the dinner.

Shaking off her thoughts, she walked past each shop, her gaze suddenly coming to a halt when she came upon a wooden shop with colourful paintings on canvas displayed elegantly in front. It was an art shop, she could see from the transparent glass, the many works of arts inside, and the brushes displayed in a far corner. It was a dream shop for artists.

When she walked in, her gaze fixated on a painting of a happy child having a picnic with his family on the grass. There was something about this painting that struck the chords in her heart. She had drawn one like this when she was little. Then, she had wanted to show her father what she had drawn only to get to his office and he was crying, head down on his desk. It had just been days since Aunt Madeline died, and, in her drawing, she'd painted Aunt Madeline white.

"Popsi, look what I drew," she told him as she stood by the door.

Her father looked at her, eyes puffed and red. "You shouldn't be here, dear. Go see your nanny."

"But I want you to see my drawing. Jadesola thinks it's beautiful. She smiled."

"I promise to check your drawing later. Popsi is busy now," he'd said.

"Popsi—"

"Holy sake, get out, Iyawa. Don't you know when someone is not in the mood?"

It was the first time he'd raised his voice, and the last time she'd seen him cry.

Iyawa let her fingers trail over the painting, feeling the texture. It was like she wanted to enter the picture, feel that moment again.

She didn't know when tears came trickling down. Along with them came the memories of her past years. The memories were already withering, but she tried to remember some things. She hadn't even drawn her own mother, and her father had shouted at her then. The face of her mother! It was still visible in her head.

It was all her father's fault. He'd kept her away from her mother all these years, and whenever she tried to talk about it, he banned her from doing so. It was like her mother didn't exist.

Wiping away her tears with the back of her palm, she knew what she needed to do. If no one wanted to talk about her mother, she was going to find answers.

Iyawa had questions. She wanted to know why her mother didn't look for her all these years. Was it because of her past? What was she doing now? Was she a cleaner or maybe she had even become rich? Why would she think Iyawa would judge her because of her past?

"Do you want to buy this painting, madam?" a cozy voice said to her.

She swerved to discover a fair-skinned, handsome guy. He seemed like he was from a mixed marriage due to his curly golden hair. Nigerian men normally didn't get hair like that.

She blinked. "Huh?"

"I asked if you wanted to buy this painting. I am the shop owner. You have been standing here for a while now."

"Oh, me? Nah. I didn't bring my card along." She smiled. "I just admire how beautiful it is. What do you call it?"

Although Jadesola's card was with her, she didn't think she wanted to buy such a beautiful painting with her younger sister's money. This painting needed to be bought with her own funds.

"Thank you. The name is 'Paradise.'" The guy squinted. "Wait a minute, aren't you the daughter of TeleInc? Iyawa? Am I dreaming? A celebrity?"

She nodded with a smile. "Yes, that's me."

His eyes gleamed with delight. "A celebrity in my shop? This is wonderful. My laptop was made from TeleInc. Best gadget ever."

"I am no celebrity. Glad you love it. Did you paint this?"

The man shook his head. "Yeah. Everything in this shop was made by me. Paradise took me weeks to finish. I am glad you like it."

"Wow. That's terrific. I make drawings, too."

"Really? That's wonderful! Do you have some sketches I can check out?"

Iyawa dipped her hands into her red bag. "Seems I brought my sketch pad with me. Phew! Here is it! I never go out without it."

The young store keeper went through her drawings page by page. "Wow, these look like some deep drawings. Like they convey emotions."

She shrugged. "Yeah. Everyone says that. It's a way of just getting away from the troubles of the world. They make me feel relaxed."

The young storekeeper smirked. "That's cool! Hey, if you ever need to make a big drawing, you can come to my store. I have lots of pencils and brushes. My name is Bamidele."

"Iyawa, as you already know. I will keep that in mind." She smiled.

"Wow! I still cannot believe you are in my shop. You really should come by sometime, and I will show you even more paintings. It's nice to know someone who understands art like you do."

She shook her head. Bamidele was tempting, if she was being sincere, but there was no way she'd go back right into the one thing that led here in the first place. "Nah, I don't think—"

He waved her off with a chuckle. "I know you are engaged. We've seen the news. Congratulations."

"Thank you, Dele. Is it okay to call you that?"

He nodded.

"I'd like to come here sometimes. And talking about friends, you could be really useful now. Could you please direct me to a boutique where I can get dinner wear?"

Bamidele's smile was infectious. "Sorry to pry, but another special occasion? I thought the marriage proposal was sweet."

She wiggled her fingers. "Yes. Matthias just has a way of surprising me. Introduction to the family is why I am getting the dinner wear."

She was good at faking things. Anyone right now would believe her. *God, forgive me for lying.*

After going to the boutique which Bamidele had directed her to, Iyawa sashayed her way out with a pink shopping bag.

Oh, how she loved shopping. It was something she and Jadesola were fond of doing once in a while when they were free from their father's workload in the office. Yes, it would be a right time to phone Jadesola.

She halted and reached for her phone in her purse, punching in some numbers.

The phone went on for two rings before someone finally picked the call.

At the sound of Jadesola's voice, she smiled. "Jadesola, you won't believe what I am doing."

Jadesola chuckled. "Good day to you, Iyawa Why do you sound so excited? Don't tell me you and Matthias finally realized you both are perfect for each other."

Iyawa resumed her trek, swinging the shopping bag in her hand. "No. That is never going to happen. Stop dreaming."

"Why? He is sooooooooooooo cute."

If there was something anyone needed to know about Jadesola? She exaggerated physical description a lot.

She thought of telling her about the challenge but didn't. Jadesola was just going to talk her out of it, and she didn't back out so easily.

"I don't think of him that way. You can have him after the engagement plan if you think he fits your taste."

Jadesola chuckled. "You know I have eyes for no one except Benjy. I just wonder when he would notice me."

Iyawa could hear some shuffling and murmurs in the background. Benjamin was a son of one of their father's best friends. He was the handsome, silent type that rarely talked and smiled a lot. Jadesola called him gentle and loveable; Iyawa called him dull.

"I do not approve of him, but you better tell him how you feel. Do you want to wake up one day and realize he is dating someone?"

Her sister gave a long sigh. "No, wait, can that happen?"

"In Yoruba movies, it does."

Jadesola laughed. "I will tell him. Not now, though. I will wait for our own story to start. What's gotten you in a good mood?"

"I am doing something we both love, and I can't just help but miss you," Iyawa said, her voice purposefully low.

She could feel Jadesola smiling through the phone. "Ah, let me guess. You went shopping, right?"

"Yeah. We are going over to his family for dinner, and there is more reason to hate my life. You know how I hate being all fake and extra polite?"

"Then just be you. Don't go extra, but do you."

"Trust me, it's going to be bad. I can't still grasp the fact that I am acting engaged. I am here for once doing something factual for the media. Why is the media not catching this now?" She huffed.

"Have you gone through your social media yet? Your proposal pictures are on all the popular blogs in Nigeria. I hate to say this, but Dad's plan might be working. Everyone was happy."

Iyawa frowned. "I don't care about everyone. They don't know me. And I just saw a fan of TeleInc. I faked happiness, and he believed it. I didn't even know I had fans."

"You see, it is easy. Keep this going for three months, and you will be free."

"That is if we don't murder one another."

Although the thoughts in her head were completely different from the conversation they were having right now, Iyawa couldn't help but think of an idea. "Jadesola, I need you to help me with something."

"What is it? Is there anything you need?" Her sister's voice was laced with concern.

"I...I don't how to say it. You might think it's not a good idea. I know—"

"Just tell me. If it isn't good, I wouldn't hold back from supporting you, but I will give you a piece of my mind," Jadesola replied.

Iyawa breathed a sigh. "I want to find my mother."

"What?"

"Look, you don't understand. You can help me get one of those spies or agents Popsi uses to fish out fraud in the company."

The shock was evident in Jadesola's voice. "You want to find your mother? Why? I don't understand."

Iyawa sighed. "Isn't it time, Jadesola? The memories keep pushing me out there, and I can't ignore it. It is like the voice calling out to that ice queen every time."

"Her name is Elsa, and Popsi won't let you. You know how he is."

"He won't know if we don't tell. I can keep it private. I just want to see her. Please, Jadesola, I need your help. She is my mother, and no matter what anyone thinks of her, I still do love her."

"Im, I don't know." There was hesitation in Jadesola's voice. "You don't think Father has his reasons?"

Walking down the street, she looked at the cars zooming down the road and frowned. "He hasn't given me any good one."

"It is going to be hard getting one of Popsi's agents. Why do you even want one of his agents? They are devoted to him."

"I find them so competent, and I don't want an agent out of Google search. Who knows who they really work for?"

"Okay. That is a good reason. I don't know how Popsi finds those agents, but I can get it out of him."

Iyawa's smile was wide. "Ah, thank you. What would I do without you?"

Jadesola laughed. "Practically nothing. You need me to survive, Iyawa. Seriously."

"Shut up."

"What type of gown did you buy for the dinner?"

She smirked. "Red."

IYAWA STOOD BEFORE the long dressing mirror in her room examining her red, one-shoulder, vintage sequined dinner gown, and of course, her dress could never be complete without her. She knew her father wanted her to beg for her bank account to be reopened, but her ego was bigger than his.

Walking down the stairs, she took a deep breath. There was Matthias all spruced up in a blue tuxedo, his hair gelled back in a fashionable way that made him desirable at the moment.

She looked at his reflection without speaking.

"You wore red."

She smiled. "I did. You hate it?"

He shook his head like he knew it was better if he didn't speak.

She swivelled around to meet his gaze.

For a moment, their eyes never left one another. Iyawa noticed how good he looked. Only from a side angle, of course. Not that she was checking him out or anything.

Matthias was the first to look away. "Look, I actually wanted to speak with you before we leave."

"Go on." She folded her arms below her breasts, her eyes never leaving him.

Pausing, he looked at her speculatively. "It's about this dinner."

"What about it?"

"My family. All my immediate family members are goanna be there, okay? And knowing my family, I just want you to take things easy with them."

Iyawa met his eyes with a frown.

"With someone else? Might not be a problem, but with you, it's like disaster. Especially with my mom," he continued.

Iyawa placed a hand to her chest in mockery. "Ouch! You hurt me with your words, Matthias."

"Iyawa, I am serious here."

"And I don't care what your family or mother thinks. And don't worry, I will handle them just fine."

SCHEMES 'N LOVE

He rubbed his forehead. "Not only that. My dad is the only one who knows about our fake-engagement."

So that's why he was looking all worried. What was the worse his mother could do to her? She had dealt with ladies like her.

"My dad knows my mom would never forgive him if she knows I got into this to save his company."

"What do you want me to do?"

"Act like we were in love, and try to avoid saying anything."

Iyawa scrunched up her face. She didn't like being told what to do, but Matthias was so sincere, she didn't know when she gave in.

"Fine. I will try, but I am not making promises."

· · ◈ · ·

THE DRIVE TO MR BADE'S mansion took less than an hour. There was this habit Iyawa had of comparing nearly every building she saw with her father's. The Bade mansion had small fences with barbed wires on it surrounding the lovely brown building.

The door was opened by a guard dressed in a sky-blue uniform.

Matthias was the first to get down, followed by Iyawa who took her strides carefully, monitoring the whole place. Outside the gates were a few journalists taking pictures as they were about to enter the building.

The guards tried blocking them from entering.

"Mr Bade Junior, is it true that you are engaged to Miss Iyawa here?" the male journalist asked, getting his pen and jotter ready.

"Yes, of course. Iyawa and I are engaged to be married soon." He leaned closer and placed his hand around her waist. "I can't wait to spend my life with her."

Iyawa managed a smile. "I love you, too, baby."

"Some people think this might be a fake plan to get the media off Miss Iyawa's back. Is this true?" the other female journalist queried.

Iyawa's smile dropped. She knew the journalist was not to be blamed as she was probably told to ask such, but still.

"I am going to meet his family now, and you think this is a stupid plan? Wake up. I'm getting married." She flashed her ring in the air purposefully to allow them to capture the moment.

Matthias shrugged. "What my fiancée said."

As they walked along the hallway, she couldn't help but admire what she did back there. The media thought they were going to take control of her? She was not going to allow them to make gossipy money out of her.

"You are getting married? Iyawa, you are more talented at acting than I am."

She propped her hands on her hips. "I don't like this. People throwing questions at me..."

"You did pretty well."

They were taken to the dining hall where she could see two people just getting settled on the antique chairs.

A woman who seemed like she was in her fifties noticed them and approached as they entered the dining room. Iyawa could see the striking resemblance between Matthias and the woman, only he was the male version. She was plump and beautiful.

"Mother," he called out. "Gosh, I've missed you."

As he enveloped his mother in a big hug, Iyawa gave a genuine smile. There was nothing sweeter than watching a mother and child's relationship. There was a time when she got injured back when she was still with her mother. She was little so the images were not clear. She didn't remember much, but she knew it ended up with her mother petting her and giving her a hug.

"I can't believe what I am seeing on blogs. You are now engaged? Why didn't I hear first?" his mother asked.

"I am so sorry, ma. I wanted to, but it might have spoiled the surprise for Iyawa."

It was then Matthias's mother finally paid attention to her. There was a look resembling repulsion.

So now, I have to deal with a wicked mother-in-law-to-be? I hate my life.

Iyawa fixed a smile. "Nice to meet you, Mrs Bade."

His mother hesitated, observing her dress. "Nice to see you, too, Iyawa. I see you've managed to charm my son into this, right, heh?"

"Mama, *Biko*."

"But why her? You know what the news says about her? Your aunties will not be happy to hear this." Matthias's mother tried whispering, but it was loud enough for everyone to hear.

Iyawa raised an eyebrow.

Mr Bade placed a hand on his wife's arm.

Yes, please tame your wife.

"Amaka, we shouldn't really bother him with such questions. They came for dinner. Let it remain like that."

Iyawa's eyes widened with surprise. *Amaka? So she is Igbo?* An Igbo woman would never let this pass. It was worse than Yoruba mothers-in-law.

His mother sighed, muttering something Iyawa made out to be, "This wouldn't have happened if you didn't take my son to meet your friend. I didn't want him to go to that party."

"But they are together now. That's what matters," Mr Bade said.

His mother snapped her fingers dramatically. "*Tufiakwa!* I didn't plan this for my son's future. He is going to be sleeping with this party girl. *She no be wife material.*"

Iyawa swallowed hard in a bid to hide her anger. She might not understand much of the Igbo language, but she knew Tufiakwa meant *God forbid*. No one was going to talk about her like that and get away with it. When would people move on?

Before she could give her a piece of her mind, Matthias led his mother to a chair, bringing out the seat for her. "Bygones are bygones, Mama. Iyawa isn't like that anymore, and for Christ's sake, she is hearing."

Iyawa's eyes threatened to frighten her fake mother-in-law-to-be as she took her seat next to Matthias.

"I am sorry about that. You know I don't care about your past. *I beg you*," he whispered to her.

"I kept my mouth shut because I said I would try. She says one more thing, and I will let your darling mother know you and your father did this for my father's money. *Make you try me*, I have no shame."

Matthias nodded, the tense lines on his face still visible.

"Why are we not eating yet?" she asked.

"My sister, Ifeoma, and her family. They are on their way."

She shifted in her seat. "You have a sister?"

Matthias's sister walked in then, and after the friction surrounding her presence, Iyawa focused on the Bade family interaction.

Ifeoma placed a kiss on her parents' cheeks as she approached the table. "Mama, Papa! I've missed you. Eii. How are you both doing?"

Mrs Bade patted her daughter's head. "I have missed you, too! Your father has been complaining about how lonely we get since you and Matthias moved out. We miss those days."

Mr Bade nodded. "It is like there is nothing much to do here anymore. The only time we get to have fun is when Ali comes for a vacation. How is my little Ali doing?"

Ifeoma's son placed a kiss on Mr Bade's cheeks.

Oh, the grandson.

Ifeoma's smile was childlike. "Mama, Papa, I got married. And Matthias is a man who we happen to know is now engaged."

Matthias's sister was a tall, glamorous lady and a replica of her mother. Her hair styled into bantu-knots seemed to convey even more of her beauty.

Mr Bade laughed and glanced at Ifeoma's husband. "Faruq, can I have my daughter back?"

Faruq shook his head, a small grin across his round face. "Sorry, but she is mine now."

Ifeoma smiled from ear to ear as she approached Iyawa.

Smile, Iyawa. She might not be bitchy like her mother.

"Whoa! You are more pretty in person. It's so nice to see you," Ifeoma said, extending her hand.

Not bad. At least, someone isn't being harsh.

Iyawa took her hand. "Me, too. You are very beautiful, I must say. Matthias said so much about you."

A lie.

"Really? I am sure he said I was very awesome, huh?"

Iyawa laughed. "Absolutely."

Another big fat lie.

"You are not as awesome as you think," Matthias said, smiling.

"Shut it, Matty. Iyawa, meet my husband, Faruq."

Faruq smiled at her. "Welcome to the family, Iyawa. It is so great to meet you."

She returned his smile. "Thank you. You have a very handsome boy."

"Ali, say hi to your aunt."

From his place on his seat, Ali gave her a shy wave.

Iyawa chuckled and waved back at him. "Hi, Ali."

Ifeoma hit Matthias on his back. "Back to you. How could you get engaged without telling us? I can't believe I missed out on planning your big proposal. I wanted to repay you." She turned to Iyawa. "You know, Matthias and Faruq planned my proposal. I work at a library, so you could understand how shocked I was when I came out to see Faruq and a ring box on a playbill."

The happiness on Ifeoma's face was so infectious. Everyone at the table was beaming.

"So Matty came in with a band playing my favourite song. Both of them managed to wow me."

Iyawa peeked at Matthias. "Baby, that was so sweet."

Matthias shrugged. "Anything for my kid sister."

Foods were brought to the table, and Iyawa wondered if this was a Thanksgiving service or just simply dinner.

The rich orange colour of Jollof rice and the familiar aroma of its leaves reached her nose, and her stomach grumbled in response. Plates of *Moi Moi* were spread out on the tables with bowls of assorted meat and fish in red stew. Chivita and 5-Alive were placed in front of everyone with glasses.

Matthias's eyes gleamed in delight. "Mama, my best food! Oh, how I've missed this."

His mother chuckled. "I made sure I prepared it myself. Now that you live alone, I doubt you even have time to prepare anything for yourself."

"Mama, I have chefs. They make my dishes for me."

"Besides, he has Iyawa now. She will prepare anything she wants for him." Ifeoma winked as she helped her son with his napkin.

Matthias's mother's smile fell from her face. "That is if she can prepare anything. She doesn't look like one who can do anything in the kitchen."

Matthias let out a heavy sigh. "Mama."

"I was only asking. Can you cook, Iyawa? It is my right to ask."

Iyawa smirked. "Of course not. Matthias knows this."

"You see. I knew it. Didn't your father get someone to teach you how to cook?" his mother asked with disdain. "A Nigerian woman who can't cook for her husband is useless."

"Mama, she will learn," Matthias said.

After moments of exchanging dagger looks with her mother, Ifeoma spoke up. "Iyawa, my brother never told us about you. Seriously, I don't get why. Matthias likes flaunting things like this."

Matthias snorted, taking a bite out of his meat. "No, I don't."

"Yes, you do. When you had your first girlfriend, you wanted us to know every little detail about her. I mean, who cares if your girlfriend likes wearing pink?"

Mr Bade laughed. "I remember it like it was yesterday. He was so happy."

"Iyawa and I just wanted to keep things private. Ask her."

Iyawa nodded. "Yeah. For personal reasons."

Matthias's mother hissed.

"Mama, stop it. They are together now. If he wants to marry Iyawa, what problems do we have with that?" Ifeoma put in.

"She is not a wife material! My son will suffer. Their kids will have a mother who can't do without nannies. Over my dead body. I can't let her in." Her eyes were burning with rage and contempt.

Iyawa flinched. What was this woman's problem with her? She had expected this, but not to this extreme.

Her eyes travelled around the table and to Ifeoma's husband who had his hands on both ears of his son like he didn't want his child to know what was happening.

"Eii. I said it's okay," Mr Bade scolded. "This is not fair."

"Please, Iyawa," Matthias whispered, his hand on hers.

She jerked away and raised her hand in surrender. She was tired of this mother-in-law and daughter-in-law rules. She wouldn't watch herself get humiliated by people who couldn't seem to keep their opinions to themselves.

Everyone waited for her to talk. Was she really going to let this woman win this argument?

She looked at Matthias. Sure, he had pleaded with her beforehand, but was she really going to accept all insult?

"Mother, I can't believe you would do this," Ifeoma said, shaking her head in slight anger.

"Can we just have a peaceful dinner?" Mr Bade's voice was now high.

Iyawa shook her head. All this shouting was giving her headache. She didn't even want to get a front seat to Matthias's family drama. *I have mine to deal with.*

She dropped her napkin and rose from her chair. "I would love to be excused."

Following a direction from the staff, she was able to make it to the corridor.

Just then, her phone lit up, which meant a message had entered.

Not again! Where are my glasses?

She pulled her phone farther from her eyes to read it. It was from the private investigator she'd hired to help find her mother.

Jadesola had spent the last few days trying to find a competent investigator and had finally found one.

The investigator had messaged her to tell her he had started on her case.

Closing her phone, she took a deep breath. Deep down, she wanted to feel hostility toward Matthias's mother, but she couldn't. Anyone would behave like that if they were in her shoes.

Staring at the sky, she wondered what she would have been if her life wasn't like this. Perhaps, she could have been a famous artist married to a wonderful man with two or three kids. Perhaps.

"I am sorry for everything. What my mother said to you was out of line. I don't know what happened to her," Matthias said behind her.

"Don't tell me you followed me all the way here? Wasn't I clear enough? I want to be excused."

Iyawa turned to face him, and for once, saw the remorseful look on his face. *Ah, I hate this look.*

She glanced away. "Don't look at me that way. I don't like it."

Matthias sighed. "I just wanted to apologize for my mother's actions. I think she isn't taking this well."

"Matthias, I understand. It's fine. Your mother isn't the first."

"And I hope she'll be the last. That was uncalled for."

"Why are you saying nice things to me?" she asked.

"Because I don't think you should be judged according to your past."

Chapter Six

Rays of sunlight caressed her face as she rubbed the sleep from her eyes with her left hand.

After last night's dinner, Matthias got her home safely. He had been pretty silent since she spoke up yesterday.

A knock came on the door.

"Who is it?"

"Madam, your father asked me to tell you that Mr Matthias is waiting for you downstairs. He said you should not keep him waiting."

She sat up on her bed, groaning. "Ooooooh. Fine, I'm coming."

This was going to be a long day.

Wearing suitable dress, she met him in the sitting room. He wore a black suit, leaning against the sofa, hands in his pockets as he watched her. This resembled a scene in one Nollywood movie she watched where a man was waiting for his wife to come down in a beautiful dress. Only she was wearing plain clothes and her hair was still messy.

She rolled her eyes. "You've got twenty seconds to tell me what you are doing here."

"You do know you look horrible now. Don't act so pretty," he said.

She glanced down at her clothes and back at him. Why was he so tall?

"Dude, you are invading my privacy. Why would a lady wake up to meet a guy she is so tired of seeing? I'm tired of seeing you every day."

"It is just eight in the morning, relax."

Iyawa felt the urge to flee.

"Shut up, Matty." She crossed her arms. "Why are you invading my privacy? I won't be nicer the next time I ask."

This time, he walked closer. "That should scare me, but we have bigger issues. You have to see this."

He handed her his phone. It was the blog of the most popular blogger in Ikeja city, Witter's. Witter had like seventeen million reads, and people believed what she always had to post.

In the blog MY VIEW ON THE ENGAGEMENT BETWEEN POPULAR PARTY GIRL, IYAWA JASETH, AND MATTHIAS BADE, Witter had made sure to tell people the engagement between them seemed fake.

"What is wrong with this Witter girl?" Iyawa straightened with a small frown. "I am not a party girl. I hate the tag."

Matthias gave her a look. "Then what are you?"

"Not a party girl."

"I feared this. If Witter doesn't believe us, I doubt many people are," he said as he towered over her.

Iyawa swallowed as she scrolled down the post. Witter had a picture of the proposal, circling Iyawa's expression on her face.

"This is nonsense! I look like I was happy at that moment."

Matthias raised an eyebrow in doubt. "You looked like the scene seemed funny to you. Who laughs at their proposal scene?"

"It is not my fault you looked stupid." She shrugged. "If I'd had a blindfold on, then I wouldn't laugh."

"Iyawa, if we want to pull this off, we need to up our game. I don't care, but we have to do anything."

She crossed her arms. "Why are you even bothered? I am the one who should be."

"You don't understand."

"Make me." She handed his phone back to him. Why should she care what Witter thought? It didn't matter as long as some believed her.

"If someone finds out this is all a sham to save your pretty face, they would want to know why I agreed to this. I can't expose my dad like that."

"Did you just call my face pretty?"

"I didn't." He gave a dismissive wave, his cheeks turning red. "Anyways, I was saying—"

"You think my face is pretty. You like me. I can sense this." A smirk tugged at her lips.

It was so relaxing to tease Matthias now and then. He thought she was pretty. She couldn't help but think he had been checking her out. Now, this sent her tummy thrilling with sensations.

Matthias puffed out his chest. "Yes, I think your face is pretty. Can I go on now?"

"Okay."

"As I was saying, if they find out why I agreed to help you, that's bad. I know you don't have any shame, but I do."

She plucked at her clothes and let out an audible groan. "What do you want me to do?"

"We go out more. You be around me, and I be around you. We start doing things together."

"Was that easy for you to say? I'm almost puked just thinking of it." She made a nauseated face. "We've been going out too much."

Matthias's head tipped back. "Iyawa, can you be serious, for once?"

"Fine. I will go out with you from now on. You happy?"

"The guts. Also, I wanted to inform you I am leaving for work. Are you going out?"

She raised an eyebrow. "That is a stupid question. We have a phone launch coming soon, and you want me to just sit here."

"Why must you turn every normal conversation into something offensive?"

"What do you all think will happen? I'll laze around, and everyone will be happy? I am going to work."

"Are you a lady? You don't ever get tired, do you? Ladies in your situation will be happy to be with me."

She smirked. "I am one of those ladies. I am a distinct one, and I won't stay in a place where I don't want to."

Matthias made to move out. "Well, good luck explaining that to your old man. Send my greetings."

· · ⚜ · ·

"GOOD MORNING, MISS Jaseth. Congratulations on your engagement," a staff said to her as she entered the elevator.

"Ah, thank you."

Stepping out of the elevator, she met another female staff.

"You looking great, Miss Iyawa. Congratulations on your engagement."

She managed a smile. "Thank you."

Slinking down the hallway leading to her sister's office, she was met with more staff who congratulated her. Jadesola's office gave a cozy feeling with low glowing lamps and touches like candles, potted plants, and a ladder to reach the high shelves. Jadesola was a nurserywoman type.

She closed the glass door and let out a sigh of relief. "My, is it Christmas today? Why is everyone happy about the engagement?"

"Why aren't you?" Jadesola swivelled in her chair, holding a paper. "Why are you just coming at this time? Dad was angry."

"When is he never angry? There was this time he got angry because I wouldn't reply him when he was talking to me."

"You made him look like a fool, Iyawa. Come on, get a seat."

Iyawa took a seat in front of her sister. "In my defence, I didn't want to make him look like a fool. Enough about Dad. How are you? And why are there so many papers on your desk?"

"You know how you advised Dad to get a new digital marketing manager and a social media manager?"

Iyawa nodded. The scene was still fresh in her head. It was their regular one-on-one session, and her father had asked for their opinions to promote their upcoming smartphone. She had asked him to get new staff.

"Yes?"

"He thinks it is a smart idea, so here I am, checking the CVs of applicants who applied for the post."

Iyawa's mouth dropped. "Wow. I thought he said we don't need more staff. He said those people were incompetent."

"Yeah, he changed his mind. If we want this phone to sell, we need diligent people."

"Hmm. What am I to do to help?"

Jadesola chuckled. "You already have a file you need to attend to. We received complaints about TeleInc ear pods. It is defective."

"What complaints? They just came out a couple months ago."

"Customers left reviews on our site. They said it makes static sounds that increase while on calls. Popsi wants you to handle it."

Iyawa knew what this meant. She had to get the technical units and offer a free get-your-ear-pods-serviced at TeleInc stores. "Okay. That sounds like so much work. I should be going then and get my team ready."

She rose from her seat.

"Wait, sit. How is Matthias? Have you guys bonded? It can help to take a break from these files."

"Would you believe me if I say nothing has happened yet? That the only thing stopping us from murdering one another is fear of God and prison?"

A smile tugged at Jadesola's lips. "You are so dramatic. Matthias is a nice guy. He helped me once when my car broke down. Just get to know him."

Iyawa stopped a few steps away from the door. "I will. Maybe if we get out of this whole drama alive."

"Drama Queen."

Iyawa pulled open the door. "Shut up."

"Don't forget to buy me lunch. Love you."

"Love you, too," she muttered.

WHEN IYAWA ARRIVED home that night, she rubbed her neck in a bid to ease the tension. Sitting in front of a computer talking to the technical team was a tedious job, and now, she just wanted to eat and sleep.

"Where is my sister?" she asked the cook who dished out her food.

"She is at the gym."

"Okay. Tell her I might join her soon.' She picked up her spoon.

The cook's fair-skinned face gleamed. "I'll tell her, ma'am."

"Okay. You can go."

Just then, her phone rang. A video call from Matthias.

Her face pulled up in a frown. She picked it up.

"Hey, Iyawa."

There was Matthias all sweaty in a blue tank top and shorts with his headset on. It was like he was laying on a blanket, and beside him was something resembling a wheel.

"Dude, why are you calling me? I'm not in the mood."

And for a moment, she thought his cheeks burned a little red.

"Hey, I just wanted to check up on you. I saw your Instagram post. You said you had a stressful day."

She looked at the screen with a sigh. "Yes. I mean, today was stressful. I had to help with some faulty gadgets, and I have neck pain from straining my neck. Why do you care?"

Matthias shrugged, and it looked like he was standing up from the ground. "Just being a good fiancé."

"That's funny. Now you can see I am fine, I should go take a nap. My neck is really bad.' She rolled her shoulders to ease her neck. That's what sitting in front of a computer all day did to the body.

He stopped her from disconnecting the call. "Wait. I...I can give tips about your neck."

She scratched an itch on her nose. "Unless you are a kind of massage expert or something, no."

"I know some exercise to relieve the pain. It is okay if you don't want my help. You look good with a stiff neck." He shrugged.

Iyawa put her head to one side.

"Okay, fine. What do you have for me?"

Matthias placed his phone in a position where she could see his full body and his surroundings. He was in the gym.

"I guess you have a gym, so let me teach you an exercise. Bend your left knee on the bench, and let the other stand on the floor."

She nodded and did as he said. "And?"

"Take this weight and bend down while you keep pulling it up and down. Can you do that?"

"I can try."

She watched as he leaned downwards, pulling the weight up and down.

"This is how you do it. Take it slow."

His voice softened her mood. When had any guy ever called her on video call? Especially to teach her now to exercise.

"Pay attention. Let your body feel that weight."

She imagined herself in his gym. She imagined how she would sniff off his mandarin orange scent.

Wait, what?

"That is enough. I want to stop."

"Why?"

She wiped her cheeks with the back of her hand. "Idiot, you are sweating, and I don't like looking at sweaty skin. Besides, I am feeling much better watching you embarrass yourself. Thanks for helping."

Matthias shook his head as if he were genuinely concerned. "I am happy to help."

And with that, Iyawa disconnected the call with just one question on her mind.

Did she just think Matthias would smell nice?

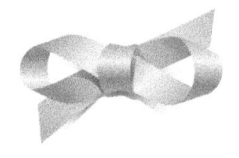

Chapter Seven

"Believe me, Iyawa, no one regrets this more than I do. I should have gotten a warning."

Iyawa's eyebrow drew upwards as a headache loomed, her feet flaring with a fiery slice of pain. "Can you just help me? I am covered in hot oil."

The kitchen smelled like burnt plantains mingled with the scent of the spaghetti on the hot plate. *And something like burnt skin.*

"How could you hold something this hot? *Nawa oo* You said you could fry plantains," Matthias said, stretching his hand to meet hers. "I doubt if any doctor could rescue these plantains."

"*Abegii.* I said I could try."

"Well, good to see you like burning skin. Just look at your feet. I think it's swollen."

Iyawa caught a glimpse of her blistered feet. It was swollen a little, and painful, too. This morning, Matthias had told her to pretend cooking a meal together and take a picture to post on their social media to make this more real. She didn't expect him to cook the spaghetti and leave her the job of frying the plantains. She couldn't blame him. He was a better cook.

It wasn't an issue until she discovered the plantains were burning. Hurriedly, she tried to remove the pan off the fire with her bare hands. Even Matthias's shouting didn't stop her. It fell and attacked her left leg. Fortunately, just a small area.

Matthias placed her arm over his neck and led her limping self out of the kitchen. He told the cook to take over and informed one other staff to bring the first aid box.

He took her first to the bathroom and washed her feet with cold water.

"*Omo,* you owe me big time *ooo*," he muttered, scooping water onto her feet. 'I don't know why I am helping."

Warmth reached her chest as she laughed and wiggled her feet. "Send my bill. Just know I won't be able to pay 'til I get my card back."

When she got to the sofa in the sitting room, she gave him an intense stare." I kind of think this is all your fault. I told you to let me cook the spaghetti."

He snickered, sitting on the stool in front of her. "Yeah, right. Like you can cook anything. You are a Nigerian—how did you escape from not knowing how to cook?"

Growing up with nannies and cooks had never resulted in her and Jadesola cooking, ever. When they grew up, Jadesola took cooking lessons, but the only lesson Iyawa took came from a Youtuber and which got her to blow up the kitchen. The sixth time.

"I didn't have a mother around to teach me, and I hate cooking lessons."

Matthias clamped his mouth shut, and something like regret filled his eyes.

He began applying one lotion onto her feet after the first aid box was brought. The way he was gentle with her feet made her achingly aware of his hard but soft hands. Sweat was trickling down his face as his eyes were fixed on her foot. The sensation was killing her.

Look away, Iyawa. Stop staring at him.

She didn't want to have such thoughts. Years ago, they had occurred, and what did he do?

"God, is the air-conditioner turned on?" He placed her feet gently on the ground. "All done. Should I send my bill?"

"What do you want? A big pretend date out? Money? Or maybe a peck on your cheeks?"

He raised an eyebrow.

She wanted to melt into the floor now, her pulse racing. This was humiliating. "I was just saying. Forget it."

Perhaps Matthias thought she was joking or not—she couldn't read anything from his expression.

"Talking about serious payments, I want you to do something for me."

She shrugged and relaxed in her seat. "Okay, but I have the right to refuse if I don't like the idea."

"Cool. I like when a lady knows how to say no."

"Okay."

He sighed, like he knew she might not like this idea. "Ifeoma and Mother are attending a wedding on Saturday, and they wanted you to come along. A girls' day out."

"What? An *Owanbe* Saturday? Why do they need me to go?"

"Because they think you will be part of the family soon. It is normal."

Iyawa raised an eyebrow in disbelief. "Your mother said that? I find it hard to believe."

"No. Just Ifeoma," Matthias said quietly.

"Your mother is going to kill me. She can't stand me. I love what you did for my feet, but I can't. Sorry, dude."

"Forget about what she thinks. If you go out with them, people will talk and think this engagement is true."

Iyawa looked at him, like she was thinking it through. "But I don't really like wedding parties."

"Why?" he asked with a suspicious stare.

"I don't just like them, but I will go."

He smiled. "That is great. Once the cook is done with the food, we will take a picture. Thank God we used my kitchen."

"What caption will you use?"

"My fiancée got burned while cooking, but I saved the day." He laughed. "I am your prince charming."

"Write that if you have a death wish."

· · ⚜ · ·

DAYS WENT BY FAST, and she buried herself in her work. TeleInc had gotten the chance to be sponsoring partners for another reality show, and Popsi congratulated her and Jadesola for a job well done. Soon, it was Saturday morning. She and Matthias hadn't really done much together since the day in the kitchen. That post had earned her an additional one thousand followers on Instagram.

It was safe to say they didn't see much of each other and said no more than greetings to one another. Right now, he had gone out with his father, and she was here preparing to meet with the females in his family. If she didn't know better, she would say it felt so real.

She grabbed her green clutch purse and looked into the mirror for the fifth time. She was wearing a green lace sequined sleeveless gown with a fancy long net draped over her shoulders and reaching the ground. Her outfit wouldn't be complete without her green gele, a headwrap worn by mostly the Igbo and Yoruba women in Nigeria, tied in layers of steps. There was no way she'd go out without a gele. As green was the colour tone used for the wedding, she was rocking it in green.

"Iyawa," Ifeoma called.

She rushed out of her room and met Ifeoma as she was climbing down the stairs. Ifeoma was also wearing green lace, but it was long-sleeved, with beautiful flower designs sewn on it.

"Saturdays are for what?"

"Parties." Iyawa laughed.

Ifeoma placed a hand over her mouth. "You look gorgeous. Just like a bride."

No one had ever told her she looked like bride material, and now, she began thinking of it. How would she look wearing a wedding gown? The only problem was she would want her gown to be red.

"Is that good? The bride should be the only bride there."

"Come on, you are wearing green, and the bride should give spotlight to you, too." Ifeoma waved her off.

As they walked out of the door, Iyawa asked," Who is getting married, if I may ask, and your mother is thrilled?"

Ifeoma laughed. "One of Mother's sophisticated friend is getting her daughter married to this rich old dude. And Mother, she isn't really thrilled about taking you along. Who cares? Finally, I get another young woman in the family who could be my soulmate."

Iyawa could feel warmth spreading through her now. "The groom is old?"

"Yes."

"How old?"

Ifeoma looked at her and nodded with a knowing smile. "Thirty years older than the bride."

"No." Iyawa burst into laughter.

Ifeoma's red Jeep was right in Matthias's driveway, and Iyawa could see Mrs Bade in the front passenger seat. Her gele was bright and big, tied in a simple style with big beads adorning her neck.

"*E kaaro ma*," she said in Yoruba.

Matthias's mother didn't even spare her a look from the front passenger's seat. All she said was, "Hmm. Look at the Jaseths' house. Still a show-off."

Ifeoma sprang the car's engine to life and turned the vehicle out of the compound. "Ma, reply very well. You said you will be nicer."

"She is greeting me in Yoruba. I am Igbo."

Well, give it to her to turn it into an inter-tribal thing.

"So where is the venue?"

Mrs Bade looked at her through the rearview mirror with a frown. "What is it with the question? You are not the one driving."

Iyawa pinned on an insolent smile. "I was just asking, ma. Is it wrong to ask?"

Mrs Bade gasped. "Did you see that smile, Ifeoma? This girl is too rude. Why bring her along?"

"Mom, she was asking a harmless question. Can you just let the lady be?" Ifeoma growled, taking a glimpse at her mother. "Banana Island, Iyawa. That's where the wedding is taking place."

An hour into the journey, and Iyawa realized something. Ifeoma was a death driver.

"Oh, my God. I need some music," Ifeoma said, stretching her hand to switch on the radio.

"Ifeoma, you are driving on high speed. Let us get to the wedding with our full bodies," her mother said.

"I think you should reduce your speed, Iffy," Iyawa put in. She wanted to go to this wedding with her body intact.

The car was soon filled with a Christian song, Ifeoma singing along.

"We aren't going to die, baby. We are going to live." She laughed.

Mrs Bade seemed unfazed, like this was a regular thing Ifeoma did.

Iyawa didn't know when she began humming along with the tune.

"Iyawa, I can hear you humming. Sing along if you know the song," Ifeoma said.

She gave a wave of dismissal. "No, I'm good. I don't really know it that well."

"Don't be fun killer. Join me. When will you have fun if not now?"

With a little reluctance at the beginning, Iyawa soon found herself singing along with Ifeoma.

The ladies burst into laughter. It felt too good to be true. This was the first time she craved the feeling of having another friend beside Jadesola. Growing up, she had a few friends, but one by one, they left, except Jadesola who loved her more than life itself.

The drive to the venue took another hour. Outside the big white hall, people in colourful attire were seen walking and taking pictures in front of cars. The majority of the colours were green with purple and gold mixing. Hawkers were seen hawking a crate of bottle water as they passed in between the guests. The smell of small chops and popcorn reached her nose, urging her stomach to cry in hunger.

On the gate of the hall was a wedding banner stating, *Welcome to the Wedding of Deola and Tope.*

As they entered the hall, guards welcomed them in and handed a wedding booklet with the picture of the couple on it. Shiny white linen with fancy lights covered the ceiling, petals all over the whole ground. People could be seen sitting around tables sporting big vases. Fuji music filled her ears as they stood before the guards.

Ifeoma snickered. "Told you the groom is old."

The groom had a white beard and looked like the father of the bride. She laughed but stopped when she saw the frown on the guard's face.

"Where can I find the seat for friends of the bride's mother?" Matthias's mother asked quickly.

The guard looked at her from head to toe. "Mother of the bride? It is right at that corner, but are you sure you are Mrs Faleti's friends? She told us to put exactly ten chairs and it's kind of filled."

"I don't understand. We are eleven in the group. You must have been mistaken." The older woman was now glancing around like she was looking for answers.

The guard went through the jotter with him. "I am sorry, ma, but you can check in with your friends if it was an error."

"Or we find another table? You don't have to sit with them. Sit with Iyawa and me," Ifeoma said gently.

"Go find a table. I am going to find out what's wrong. I donated one million to this wedding so I can sit on that seat." And with that, the older woman sashayed her way into the other end of the hall.

When Iyawa and Ifeoma found a seat, Iyawa couldn't take her eyes off Matthias's mother who had already reached the table and was talking to one of her friends.

"Don't worry about Mother. She would never see what we are all seeing." Ifeoma followed her gaze.

Iyawa tilted her head to the side. "I am curious. Why didn't they add her name? Aren't they friends? And why aren't they wearing green like everyone else?"

"Yes and no."

"Huh?" Iyawa looked at Ifeoma who was putting a puff-puff to her mouth.

Ifeoma paused to chew. "They don't really like Mom. They think they are more sophisticated than she is. They met at a party like this. I try telling her, but she thinks they like her. I seriously don't know why they are wearing purple lace."

It finally clicked. Bullying at an old age like this? Well, she wasn't surprised. Nigerian owanbe mothers loved hanging out with someone who fitted their taste, and sadly, her own fake mother-in-law-to-be was going to be put down by her friends.

The noise at the other end started to increase just a bit. Mrs Bade was shouting words she couldn't hear due to the Fuji song over the speaker. Everyone was now staring at them in wonder.

A woman in purple lace and gele stood up to her, poking her hand as she shouted, too.

Iyawa nudged Ifeoma. She didn't like the older woman's attitude to her, but she didn't hate her enough to let everyone watch her this way. "Whoa. It is getting heated. We should do something."

Ifeoma widened her eyes. "Oh my God. I don't know what to do. They do this sometimes. I can't fight. Mother won't like me interfering."

Iyawa rose from her seat. "That is not my problem. I was born to fight."

She dropped her purse on the table and rushed to the scene, not minding if Ifeoma was following her.

"Iyawa, wait, please."

As she approached, she could hear Matthias's mother saying, "You said the colour was green for everyone. Why didn't you tell me friends of the bride's mothers are wearing purple?"

The woman pushed her a little. "Amaka, you should really stop making a scene now. Everyone is watching."

"No, you tell me why my mother-in-law-to-be isn't allowed to sit here," Iyawa said.

"This doesn't concern you. I told both of you to sit," Mrs Bade replied.

A brown-skinned lady from the table turned her eyes to her. "And you are?"

"Her daughter-in-law-to-be."

The woman cackled. "Oh, yeah. She told us about you. The spoilt bride for a wife. Thank God, you finally decided to settle down. No one was really going to marry you, anyways."

"You don't talk to people like that." Ifeoma held Iyawa's hand.

"Ifeoma, take her and leave here. This is not your business."

Iyawa stood in front of Amaka, gently pushing the older woman back. She began removing her earrings. "It is now. I am going to show this woman why they call me black sheep."

"What do you think you are doing?" Mrs Bade asked. "You this girl and your wahala. These are my friends. I can handle them."

"Friends?" Iyawa scoffed. "These people aren't even the friendliest with you, and everyone can see. From afar, I could tell these people don't like you, and that is why I am here to put her in her place."

Iyawa turned to the woman whose smug look was still intact. "Let me guess, you must be the mother of the bride. You have a really big audacity for someone marrying off her daughter to a man old enough to be your father. I mean, come on. Just because everyone here is acting like they don't see it doesn't mean we are blind."

"I don't know what you are talking about. Times have changed. Age is just a number."

That elicited a burst of laughter from Iyawa. "Please. Don't even come with that bullshit. You sold your daughter for the money, we know. I mean, you didn't pay a dime in this wedding arrangement because if you did, you wouldn't be concerned about who is sitting where at a wedding. You would be busy with other things like making your daughter okay and comfortable in this big stage for her which I must say, I feel real pity for her for having a kind of mother like you. It must have been really tough growing up."

"You whore. How dare you storm into my daughter's wedding and insult me like this? I will have you thrown out of here. You and your beggar of a mother-in-law. We never really liked her anyway. God, she was always a bother."

Mrs Bade gasped, and at that moment, Iyawa felt pity for her.

"At least Mama Amaka never put her interests first before her children, much less her daughter!"

Sounds of approval rose from the table, and some of the women were now giving the mother of the bride the side-eye. One woman even stood up and left.

"Come on, Mummy," Iyawa said. "Let's get out of here."

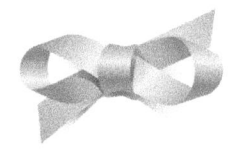

Chapter Eight

That morning, Iyawa had a weird dream. At first, she was with Matthias in a garden full of flowers.

They were arguing about something. She couldn't remember the details, but she remembered him pulling her for a kiss. In the middle of an argument.

She swung her warm feet out of bed and into cold slippers. Thank goodness, she didn't finish the dream. Dream Matthias had been about to kiss her, and worse, she couldn't stop thinking of it.

She was so tired of this game happening between them. All this fake engagement stuff needed to take main priority now.

This is all because I am too nice.

She knocked on her sister's door. "Sleepy beauty. Wake up. Today is Saturday."

"I am not done sleeping," Jadesola said.

When she came out of the room and down the hallway, everywhere was silent. It was like there was nobody at home. Of course, her father had a habit of leaving very early for work. Like he was scared of being sacked or whatever.

A growl from her stomach stopped her in her tracks. She needed to snack on something. Food, something peppery.

Iyawa made her way to the kitchen and met a young man and a lady, both dressed in white chef outfits.

She inspected the kitchen. It was big enough and beautiful, with its patterned linoleum flooring. Different types of appliances like a dishwasher, a fridge, a stove, and a microwave were all present in white.

She could hear the hiss from the coffee maker, and the steam wafting up from a pot of boiling rice reached her nostrils. Her stomach grumbled like it could smell the rice also.

She sat on the stool in front of the counter, tapping her fingers on the surface. As soon as the food was done, she ate to her satisfaction.

"Can I ask you a question?" she said to the female chef who was clearing the dishes.

The female chef blinked. "Ma'am?"

"You are such a good cook. I enjoyed what I ate now. Would you offer to teach me how to cook?"

She had been thinking about it. If she ever wanted to get married to a Nigerian guy, she needed to know her way around in the kitchen. Besides, it would be better to prepare something for herself once in a while.

"Ma'am. You want us to teach you how to cook?" The lady pointed at her other colleague.

Iyawa narrowed her eyes at the male chef. "Not him, though. Dude has been staring at my nightwear for a long time now. That's creepy."

"Ma...No...I swear, I wasn't looking." His gaze was now facing the floor.

"Oh, come on, Iyawa. Stop stressing the poor guy."

Iyawa swirled on the stool and pulled on a wide smile when she saw her sister. "Oh, look who is here. The sister who is done sleeping."

Jadesola stood at the kitchen door. She wore brown pants with a white top and slippers. Jadesola was always beautiful.

Her sister waved a hand of dismissal. "Now, don't be dramatic. And what are you doing in the kitchen? Blowing something up? Dad's insurance can't save your cooking."

"Ha ha. So funny. Now who is being dramatic?" Iyawa said dryly. She turned to the female chef. "What do you say?"

The other woman nodded. "Okay, ma'am. Just let me know when."

"Sure, but one thing, don't let my father know, okay?"

"Okay, ma."

Jadesola's eyes widened. "Im, I heard you are taking cooking lessons. Why now, if I may ask?"

Iyawa rose from the stool and led the way to the sitting room. "Sweetie, what are you thinking?"

"That you are doing this because of him. I don't know why, but I am sure it is because of him."

"No. Jadesola, I know it is hard to believe, but we hate each other's guts. I once kneed him in the groin because he was annoying." She shrugged half-heartedly.

Jadesola's mouth slacked. "I don't know what to say to you. Seriously." Her sister's expression turned serious. "Those agents I got for you came back with results."

"What? That is great news. Did they find my mother?" Iyawa sat up on the sofa, her body temperature rising.

"Iyawa, relax. Okay. Look—"

"Don't you use that tone with me. What is wrong with my mother?" Her voice was now breaking. What if the worst had happened to her mom? She shuddered inwardly at the thought of possible things to have happened. "Did my mother die? How long? Did she at least have a befitting burial site?"

"What? No. Your mother isn't dead."

She looked at her sister in confusion. "Then where is she? Is she here in Nigeria?"

"South Africa. Your mother is in South Africa." Jadesola dipped her hand into her pocket and handed the paper to Iyawa. "This is the address."

Jadesola's expression still made her hesitate to collect the paper. It sent her mind spinning. In half curiosity and half happiness, she asked," And?"

Jadesola boldly met her eyes. "She has a family now."

She drew a deep breath. It was better she grasped on to reality. This was who her mother was, and she wanted her anyways.

"That's good. God, I am so glad she is still alive. You know what this means? I am going to South Africa, Jadesola."

Jadesola's black eyes became unreadable. "You should not go, Iyawa. What if Dad knows what you are about to do?"

"He won't know. I would think of something before then, but the thing is, I am going."

Iyawa didn't understand why Jadesola wasn't happy for her. Was it because of her mother's profession?

"What if he finds out?"

"Are you going to tell Popsi, Jadesola?" Jadesola kept her expression together, but Iyawa knew better. "You don't want me to go find my mother? I can't believe you will tell on me. Here I was, thinking you are on my side."

"I didn't say—"

"Go on. Tell him. You've always had his undying love, and now, you are going to ruin my chance of finding mine."

Jadesola's face had a touch of sadness, tears filling up her eyes. "Yes, I don't want you to go."

Iyawa felt her heart shatter into pieces. This was her sister and only best friend saying such words to her.

"I don't want you to go because I fear you might not come back after meeting your mom." Jadesola sobbed.

Iyawa's expression broke into a sad smile. "Oh, Jadesola. You think I will ever leave you?"

"You are more than a sister to me. You are my soulmate. If you leave, who would I gossip with? Who would I do things with?"

Iyawa used her hand to clean her sister's tears. Thinking of it now, she knew she couldn't live without Jadesola. This lady was like a part of her.

"I didn't know you felt that way. Why didn't you tell me?"

Jadesola sniffed. "I didn't want to be the one who stops you from meeting your mother."

Iyawa paused, her thoughts running through her head. "Look, I will come back. I promise you."

"Iyawa, don't joke with me. Are you serious?"

She nodded. "I am serious. I promise you I will come back, and you will be the first person I will first see."

"I love you so much." Jadesola enveloped her in a tight hug.

"Heaven knows you are the best gift I have ever received."

· · ~ · ·

AFTER JADESOLA HAD left to go do something, Iyawa treated herself to a nice, long soak in the bathtub, different ideas spanning over and over as she held the paper containing the address. South Africa was very far from Nigeria. If she wanted her father to believe her, she had to think bigger.

She relaxed deep into the water, her head resting on the tiles of the bathtub. Ah, how she missed just sitting in a bathtub and doing nothing. Deep down, she craved going back to her lifestyle. If she wasn't fake-engaged to Matthias now, she would have been doing different things for herself.

Iyawa reached for the glass of lemon juice on the table beside the bathtub but paused when a plan came to her mind. She quickly called a number, the ringing sound surging through the speaker.

"Some of us are busy on Saturdays," his groggy voice said.

She tilted her head to look at her phone. "Would you relax? I am sure you're just waking up."

There was a pause and then some shuffling. "You ain't wrong. So I assumed the call was urgent. This isn't."

She gave him a smile even if he couldn't see it. "It is urgent."

"Speak up."

"I need your help. You owe me, remember?"

"Yes?"

"As much as this disgusts me to say and I am serious, I did a lot of thinking. I would like us to go on a mini-vacation."

He paused, like he could not believe what he was hearing. "What?"

"A mini-vacation," she repeated.

"You and me? You are serious? That is a death wish."

"Do I sound like I am joking to you? I am serious. Let's go on a mini-vacation."

"Ask for something that doesn't sound like a death wish."

Iyawa frowned. "I want to go on this vacation because I want to find my mother. I shouldn't be explaining this to you since you owe me, but yeah, I want to find my mother."

There was movement in the background. "Uh. Where?"

"South Africa. I have the address on this paper."

"What about your father? How are we going to tell him we are going on a vacation?"

"He will do anything for the company. I have a plan, but first, are you in?"

"You think I will refuse after what you did for my mom? No."

. . ⚜ . .

"I DON'T UNDERSTAND you two. Who is this Witter girl?" her father asked, his eyebrows raised inquiringly.

There was something about her father's office that screamed authority. With shades of black and white and posters of TeleInc products on the wall, it seemed quite dull.

"Witter has a blog and—"

"She knows we are faking it. I can show you a snapshot of what she wrote on her blog," Iyawa said quickly.

Her father squinted, gaze going between Matthias and her. "Matthias, is that true? Is this Witter girl really worth our worries? The news already believes you are together."

"Yes, sir. I was the one who showed it to Iyawa. Witter has lots of followers, and I fear her followers would believe what she says. Yes, the media has a say, but soon, they will start looking for reasons not to believe this."

"And you know what will be more shameful? That we tricked the media. We would be all over the news, and everyone will laugh at us. People won't ever believe a word we say."

Iyawa relaxed in her seat. She knew she'd gotten to her father. His reputation in the media was very dear to him. He wouldn't want people to think otherwise of him.

Her father gulped. "Well, you two seem like you have a plan. What plan, except breaking this scheme up, do you have? And let it be a reasonable one, please."

"Let us take a mini-vacation," Matthias said. "It is the only way for people to think it is real."

"A mini-vacation? That is absurd. Everything is absurd."

"Sir—"

"I know my daughter well, Matthias. She would never be okay with this plan unless she has something in mind." Her father pointed to her. "What did she threaten you with?"

This man was never going to believe her. He knew when she was lying and joking. It was like she was another version of him she really could read. If she wanted to visit her mother, she had to put more lies in.

Iyawa snorted. "Great, Dad. Nice to see you still think bad about me. Here I am, trying to make amends for things I did, and you are not giving me the chance to."

For a moment, she thought his face softened.

"Okay. Let us say I agree to this ridiculous idea. Where did you want to go? How many days?"

Iyawa wondered if she should say the place? What if the old man knew where her mother was?

"South Africa," Matthias said before she could finish thinking. "Two weeks."

She resisted the urge to pat his back. She'd told him what to say, and he was doing it very well.

Her father's eyes rested on her. "South Africa? Why South Africa? What happened to Spain? UK? The US?"

"I have been to those countries. Besides, I have heard so much about South Africa. I want to go there. This way, everyone would believe us," she finished. "Couples going on a mini-vacation."

"Is Jadesola aware?" her father asked.

"Yes."

The old man relaxed in his seat. "It sounds like a good plan. Okay, I will pay for your tickets and all. Just send me the bill, Iyawa."

"Yes, Popsi." She smiled.

"And Matthias? Thank you for helping my daughter."

Everything else got blocked out, but the only thing to register was the fact she was going to see her mother.

Chapter Nine

No one had said excitement felt like this. Two days passed, and the joy at the fact she was going to meet her mother knew no bounds. Just this morning, she had packed her things into a big pink suitcase. The only problem was it wouldn't lock because it was too full. There was nothing she wanted to leave behind. She needed everything in this box if she was going to survive on this mission.

She had called Jadesola last night to her room, and both sisters had almost cried as they packed her luggage. Iyawa pushed the suitcase down again, attempting to lock it, but it proved futile.

"Stupid suitcase."

"Ouch! The suitcase did nothing wrong."

At the sound of his voice, she turned to the door frame. Matthias was dressed in a black polo shirt with white edges and navy shorts. Her gaze got subtly drowned in his physique. She needed to know why he affected her this way.

She gave him a brutal stare. "What are you doing in my room?"

"Jadesola said I could come in. Your room looks weird."

"Forget about my room. I can't close the foolish suitcase."

"Then reduce the stuff in it."

"Your comment wasn't needed."

He shook his head, chuckling. "Can I help with the suitcase?"

"I didn't say I needed your help. A lady can do what a man can do."

"Yeah. I can see you are doing just fine with it." His mouth curved in pure mockery.

Iyawa huffed and waved her hand in a gesture of dismissal. "Whatever. This suitcase is driving me nuts. Do your thing, let's see."

She watched as he worked his magic and clamped the suitcase shut.

"Say thank you." He smiled with satisfaction.

She scoffed. "It was so easy."

"You are welcome."

"I didn't say thank you."

He chuckled. His gaze slid from her face to her body, and he studied her with curious intensity.

She glanced down at her outfit. She was dressed in a multi-colour Ankara jumpsuit. Matthias's eyes bathed her in admiration.

Men would always stare. Even the not-so-innocent ones.

"Stop staring. You look stupid," she hissed as she grabbed her suitcase.

He laughed. "If it were up to you, I'd always look stupid. Let me help you with this. Mine is already in the car."

"You won't win this challenge by being sweet. I am not that easy."

"I was just helping, Iyawa. Don't read meaning to it."

She flattened her palms against her cloth. "Where do we stay in South Africa? We haven't made any arrangements."

"I have all that settled already. I hope you see I am all the man you need."

When they got out of the house, they met the chauffeur waiting by Matthias's car.

The drive to the airport was quiet and long. The chauffeur helped Iyawa get her luggage down and pulled it into the airport, leading the way while Matthias rolled his behind him.

The automated door at the entrance opened. Iyawa could see gates for many airlines, uniformed staff attending to people, and signs from the ceiling directing passengers to different areas of the airport.

Matthias brought out their boarding passes and form of his passport and even hers as they headed to security.

She lowered her gaze. "How did you even get my passport?"

He shrugged. "Jadesola helped me. And with your father's money, it was easy to get us a boarding pass."

"Awn. You are such a thoughtful fiancé."

The sound of a female voice announcing the arrival of an airplane interrupted her.

They met with a TSA agent who checked their boarding passes and passport. Afterward, their belongings were placed in bins and sent through an X-ray machine while they were being checked in a separate machine scanning their bodies.

It was then the chauffeur bowed to announce his departure. Iyawa repacked her luggage, and Matthias led the way to the correct terminal.

They soon settled onto the plane, and the flight attendant helped with their luggage. It took a while before the plane took off.

Matthias handed her a flyer. "Check it out. That's where we are going to stay while we find your mother."

She inspected the green-coloured flyer. "Bab's town? That's where we are going?"

He gave a brief nod as he relaxed into his seat. "Yes. We are lodging at a famous hotel there. My friend owns it."

"You said we? Are you planning on helping me?"

"Isn't that why you took me along? I thought you needed my help."

She shrugged. "I didn't have anywhere to put you as we are in this fake thing so you had to follow me. Thanks for wanting to help. I appreciate it, even though I would not be able to pay you back."

"It is fine. Why don't we take a picture now and post it later?"

Iyawa nodded. After taking sweet pictures together, they began doing different things on their phones.

"I still can't believe your father fell for that. I am still scared. What if he finds out why we took this vacation?" Matthias asked.

"If there is one thing about that man, he is scared of what people think of him."

While growing up, he'd made her and Jadesola realize they must not do anything that would jeopardize their reputation. It was a rule she broke often.

"What happened between you and your father?" Matthias asked carefully. "You guys have this love-hate relationship?"

Pride kept her from saying how she, too, was confused about the whole thing, so she muttered a reply. "I don't know when, but it just happened."

"Why didn't you want him to know about your mother in South Africa?"

The line of her mouth tightened. "Yeah, right! If my father is involved, he would make sure I don't go for this vacation. I've lost my account, and I can't afford to lose my only chance to meet my mother."

Matthias closed his eyes, head still leaned backward. "Do you really like SA like you told him?"

"I have never been there. Besides, If I were to jump on another plane now going to Paris, I would gladly go."

"You like Paris?" he asked.

"I live for Paris. I have also never been to Paris 'coz Popsi doesn't let me travel so much. I wish to go."

Ever since she was little, she had always loved Paris. Even her mother knew how much Paris meant to her. The first day she fell in love with Paris was when she watched a cartoon about travelling there. She had been hooked since then. Matthias wouldn't understand her love for Paris—she couldn't tell him the obsession grew from a cartoon.

His eyes grew openly amused. "Do I have a country I so wish to go? Yes, yes. Spain. I want to go to Spain."

"Spain?"

He nodded. "Yeah, Spain."

"You are kidding. Why would you want to go to Spain?"

He shrugged. "I don't know. I love the way they speak. It is intriguing."

"Can you speak Spanish, Matthias?" She chuckled.

"No. You can speak Español right?"

"How did you know that?"

He shrugged dismissively. "When we first met, you said Hola and some other thing I can't remember."

She rolled her eyes in hatred for that day. How could he still remember what she had said, and how dare he speak of it?

"I speak Spanish. We had people from Spain that day. Dad paid a teacher to give me Spanish lessons when he was about to sign a deal with business partners from Spain. He used it to lure them." She smoothed her hair with her hand.

Her mind wafted to those days of her and her father's very strict business relationship. Whenever they were to seal a big international deal, he had a rule. One of them had to find a way to learn the language of the other person. She could speak Spanish while Jadesola could speak French. Only her sister had been to Paris.

Matthias's laughter floated up from his throat. "Wow, that is very good, baby. I am proud of you."

"Don't call me baby."

"Say something, then."

"Huh?"

"I want you to say something in Spanish." He was pleading with his eyes.

She almost met those eyes. "No. I am not going to do that."

"Please. Just say something in Spanish."

"No, Matthias."

"Yes."

"No. Would you just grow up?" She furrowed her brows.

"Yes. If you say just one sentence in Spanish."

"*Estas Loco,* Matthias."

He gave a smug smile. "Wow, what does it mean?"

"Why do you want to know? You said to speak in Spanish, not interpret."

He winked when he caught her eyes. "*Estas Loca*, Iyawa. *Estas Loca.*"

Her mouth dropped. "You...You—"

"Yes. I can understand. If I like Spain so much, you should know I would try and learn their language. I'm not that good, and there are some certain words I don't understand, but *Estas Loco*? Seriously?"

She lifted her chin. "Well, you are crazy, that's no lie. Telling me to speak Spanish when you can also speak is insane."

"I knew you would say something mean. You always do."

"Well, I am Iyawa, aren't I?" she added with a slight smile of defiance.

Matthias shook his head. "Yes, you are."

Iyawa couldn't believe she'd just had a conversation with Matthias. Not just a conversation, but one she didn't hate. It was like they were conversing without putting their worries in between.

When they got out of the plane, there was a black Rolls-Royce car waiting just for them in front of the airport.

Matthias shook hands with the driver who was dressed in black suit. "From Rari?"

The driver nodded and assisted them with their luggage.

"So how do you know this Rari guy? A business partner or what?" she asked when they settled in the car.

"We went to the same high school and college in Nigeria. We've been best friends for a long time now."

She raised an eyebrow. "People still stay in touch with their high school mates? I don't even have the number of my friends in college."

She couldn't remember the last time she'd seen her high school friends. She could remember they weren't really friends per se but people who loved partying.

"Yes. Rari and I stayed in touch all through."

"And why is he here and you are in Nigeria?"

Matthias rolled his eyes. "Because he has his own life, Iyawa. His father lives in South Africa. He came here to help him oversee their hotels. He is married now."

"And his name is Rari?"

Matthias shook his head. "Yes. That is his name."

"Who name their kids Rari? What does it mean?" She snickered.

"My bad. His full name is Ferrari."

Iyawa's mouth dropped. "Kill me now. Ferrari as in the car?"

Matthias chuckled. "Yes. His mother loved the name Ferrari and decided he was deemed to bear the name. It's bizarre, but I love it."

"So, you are the type of father who would give his kid such a name? Lemme guess, your first child will be Toyota Bade."

"No. Toyota is a bad name for a child. Rari, I just think it is a cool name."

She scoffed. "It is bad. Very bad. It's like his parents didn't know what to name him, and all they had to do was look at their Ferrari and be like, that would be a good name."

The drive to the hotel took about thirty minutes, and the car halted in front of an elegant building.

The hotel was a perfect array of laidback hues. It gave a sense of home away from home, of a place of nurturing safety. Wow, this was giving her reasons why she should love this vacation.

When they got down, Iyawa saw a dark-skinned, slender, clean-looking man in a suit waiting by the entrance. He stood as if he prided himself on his good looks.

Before she could even say anything, she felt Matthias's arms firmly on her waist, and she had the wildest urge to jump back.

"Erm... Hello, what do you think you are doing?" she whispered as they approached the man by the entrance.

Matthias let out a breath. "Please, just play along. I beg you. I will explain later."

A part of her wanted to disregard him, but there was another part pushing her to just play along.

She held her fists bunched at her sides.

"Matthias, my dear." The man's lips parted in a display of straight white teeth.

"Rari, how are you, bro?" Matthias greeted as he exchanged hugs with Rari.

When they withdrew from the hug, Rari glanced at Iyawa. "And I am sure this is your beautiful fiancée over here. You are right. She is very pretty."

Iyawa gave a knowing smile. "The name is Iyawa. Nice to meet you, Rari."

Rami stretched forth his hand.

"You are very beautiful. Matthias must be so lucky to have someone as beautiful as you," he said. "He wouldn't stop talking about how great you are."

Iyawa chuckled. "Oh, baby. You didn't have to."

"Dude, how is your Zola? I don't see her anywhere," Matthias said hastily.

Rari blushed. "Ah, Zola couldn't make it today, but she promised to come meet you and your fiancée tomorrow. She has been expecting you two."

"Sure, bro, it's been a long time since we've seen each other. How many years now?" Matthias asked.

"Five years, dude. Why don't I let a staff take you to your room, and we can catch up later? Do not want to keep Iyawa waiting."

Rari called on a bell boy who assisted with their luggage and handed a card to Matthias. "I got you the best room as you required. Enjoy your stay in SA."

Matthias smiled as he shook Rari's hand. "Thanks, bro. We will catch up later in the day."

"Just ask the receptionist if you need me."

When they got to the entrance of their room on the second floor, Matthias slid the smooth plastic card into the slot and then yanked it out to disengage the lock. After he tipped the bell boy and they had entered the room, Iyawa flopped unto the bed with a grateful sigh.

She watched as Matthias stood and pushed his hands deep into his pockets.

"Can you explain what just happened down there? You were eager to pretend in front of your friend."

Matthias straightened and sighed loudly. "I am sorry I had to force you to do that."

"You didn't want your friend to know we aren't a real couple? That all this is a sham to help your father's company get the money it needs to settle its debt?" Her mouth pulled into a cynical twist.

"Or that we are doing this to help you," he said.

She pulled on a cheesy grin.

Matthias slid onto the red cushion chair. "The problem is, I don't want him to know."

"What? I thought you were the big nice guy who doesn't give a care about this sham engagement."

"I don't. I accepted to do this with *my full chest*. If Rari knows I did this to help my father, he is going to lecture me. And I don't want to be lectured. At least not from someone I don't really know."

Iyawa slanted her brow, looking at him in a way that made sure to tell him she didn't understand what he was getting at. "Now tell me why I shouldn't expose you in front of your friend after what you just told me."

"Because even you can be persuaded."

She hissed. "I don't have time for your drama. I need to rest, and I must say, this hotel is beautiful."

"Are we sharing the same bed?" he asked.

She sat up on the bed. "There is only one bed. I just noticed."

"It's fine. I will take the floor. Just throw me a blanket and a pillow. I'm good."

His smile made her skin tingle.

"Wow. That's so gentle of you. You came here to help me, yet you keep trying to be nice."

Matthias shrugged. "I am a good man."

She chuckled as she relaxed on the bed. "Well, happy back pain to you."

She didn't hear his reply, but she could hear him muttering some words in the background, and before she knew it, darkness clouded her vision.

· · ∽✿∾ · ·

WHEN IYAWA WOKE UP the next morning, she wasn't expecting the two things that happened to her. The first problem? Matthias was snoring, and he had his hands around his pillow along with his right leg. His chest rose and fell as he snored. It was like she could hear his heartbeat. The second problem? She couldn't help but notice it was miserably cold in the bedroom. Like she was freezing.

She sat up, the cover that had protected her from the fierce, cold night air falling on the ground. She picked her pillow and threw it at him. Her face was hot, and she avoided his gaze as he tried to come out of his sleepy state.

"Who did that?"

Iyawa rubbed her fingers together. There was this achy, feverish feeling spiralling through her. She sneezed so hard, droplets fell on her hand.

"Do you have a cold?" he asked, rubbing his eyes.

God, she was sneezing. Her mouth twisted at the heavy thumping going up in her head. "And my head is pounding. Why were you snoring? Where is my pillow?"

"Ha-ha. That's funny. I don't snore. Also, you threw your pillow at me."

"No, I didn't." She sneezed again.

She could hear the low hum of the air conditioner. The room was so cool, one would think it had been turned up to max.

"Where is the remote? I am not going to freeze here."

She felt another sneeze coming and frantically reached for her purse on the bedside stool. But a violent sneeze ripped through her lungs so fast, she barely had time to cover her mouth with her hand.

Matthias reached the bed and touched her shoulder. "Are you good?"

"Switch off the air conditioner, Matthias."

He jolted upright and reached for the remote control on the bedside table, and after he'd switched it off, he settled next to her. He pushed tendrils of her hair away from her face, and his hand laid on her forehead.

"You have a bit of a temperature," he said. "How did you catch a cold?

Iyawa breathed. The warmth of his hand was doing so much to her. His hand was lingering too much.

Hastily, she drew his hand away. "I am fine. Give it an hour or so, it will be better."

She was so wrong. It didn't get better. From sneezing, it had upgraded to coughs. Her throat was dry like a desert.

"I am waiting for when it gets better," Matthias said, looking down at her, an hour later.

Iyawa groaned. She was still on the bed, in a lotus position, with a big cover draped over her. She stared back at Matthias who was now sitting on the edge of the bed watching her. She wasn't used to having this much attention around her. Whenever she was sick, it was either Jadesola helping her with the medicines or she visited the clinic. Why was he being so caring?

He shook his head disapprovingly. "You are not getting any better now, are you? I promise, if you die—"

She leaned her head back. "I...I can manage. Don't you have anywhere to go? Like, just go do your thing and let me be."

He frowned. "We are supposed to find your mother. And leave you here all by yourself? What if anything happens to you?"

"I am fine, Matthias. It is just cold. Have you never gotten a cold?"

"Just cold, you say? Did you even hear your own voice now? You sound like the old woman who gave Snow White a poisoned apple."

She cleared her throat. He wasn't going to give up.

Men and their dramas.

"Look, here is what will happen. Your body needs rest, so I think I will order a bowl of hot chicken soup because you definitely need it."

"Chicken soup?" she asked. "What would it do?"

He gave a shrug. "It is really good when you have a cold. My mom cooks it a lot for me when I am sick and down with cold. For the moment, you will take it, and I will find a pharmacy where I can get an OTC for you or a pain reliever for your headache."

"Why are you helping me again?"

"Are you serious? It's about me trying to help you so I and others won't get infected. But the point is, I am trying to help you. So please, let me just do it."

She stared at him like he had grown horns. "Is this a way of winning the challenge? You think you can win me over by doing this?"

Matthias raised his hand in surrender. "Not now, Iyawa."

"Fine." She sighed.

When he left and came back thirty minutes later, she was sipping the soup he had ordered for her.

"Hey," he said, closing the door before him.

She shook her head in response. Her throat was feeling so much better now.

He settled onto the red cushion. "Look, I found you the drugs to help. Are you better now?"

"My throat doesn't feel clogged anymore. And the drugs, thank you."

"Yeah. I told you. I also don't want to catch the cold. I'm worse when I am down with a cold. So where did you get a cold from? Is it the air conditioner? You should have asked me to reduce it last night," he added.

Iyawa took another spoon of the soup, ignoring him. Why was he helping her? How was she even enjoying the fact Matthias was paying attention to her? This was crazy. Crazy, but she secretly liked it.

He shook his head. "You are going to be better by tomorrow, and then we can go to that address."

"Matthias," she called.

He looked at her, his eyes searching hers. "Yes?"

"Thank you."

He smiled genuinely. "Don't worry. I was born a gentleman."

• • ⚜ • •

THE NEXT MORNING, MATTHIAS borrowed Rari's car, and soon, they were out looking for Iyawa's mother. They had passed civilization, and all they could see were tall trees and grasses.

"Did you ask Rari about the address? Is this the right address?" Iyawa chew on a cuticle.

Matthias nodded, not taking his gaze from the road. "Yes. I asked him. The journey is a long one, so you better sit tight."

"Well, what did he say? Can we make it today? How many hours' journey are we going on? Why is our car the only vehicle taking this route?"

Matthias sighed. "Relax, Iyawa. Rari said it is a long journey from here, but we should be able to make it by evening or the next day."

"Did you just say the next day? Why didn't we take a plane? Please, tell me you know a shortcut."

"No, I don't. I don't live in SA, remember? I can't risk taking a shortcut."

"But—"

"Just be patient. We will get there in the evening."

Her mouth twisted wryly. "Evening? Matthias, I will die of anxiety. This place is looking so deserted and creepy. I am starting to think this is a wrong address."

"Wasn't it an agent who got it for you?"

"Yes?"

"Then you can start by relaxing. We will still meet your mother no matter what you do. Don't stress it."

The glow of his smile warmed her.

She nodded. "That is true. I...I am just so nervous. It's like the car cannot go any faster."

"Iyawa, I don't mean to intrude, but how many years has it been since she was gone?" He stole a glance at her.

Her mind raced to the image of her younger version crying out for her mother. She was so little then. How could a five-year-old girl understand what was happening then?

She let out a deep breath. "My mother wasn't gone. I was taken away from her."

"That is the same thing, Iyawa. She wasn't with you while you were growing up. I don't know why you think rephrasing it makes it sound different."

"Excuse you?" Her voice was shakier than she would have liked.

Matthias let out a shrug. "I am just saying. Your father told my father that your mother left you. I mean—

Iyawa's smile fell. "Of course my father did. Everyone believes that man. Matthias, my father is a liar. He took me away from my mother. How could I believe anything he says?"

"Why didn't your mother come look for you, then? If truly your father took you away from her, she should have searched for you?" Matthias said.

Iyawa's eyes narrowed suspiciously. If he supported her father so much, why was he here pretending to help her?

"What would you have her do? I don't know if you have forgotten, my father is a powerful person who thinks he can fix anything with his ideas and money. Do you think he would have allowed her to gain my custody?" Her voice was laced with cold.

"Im, I just don't want you to make decisions without—"

She raised a hand, her expression tight with strain "Enough, Matthias. You know nothing about my mother, and I will not allow another word of accusation against her."

He frowned. "Wait, I wasn't—"

"I said, enough. If you know you don't approve of my mother so much, why are you even helping?" She paused and turned to look at him. "Jesus, don't tell me you are still spying for my dad because what on Earth, Matthias?"

"How can you even say that? I am helping you because I want to and not because of your father. How can you even say that about me?"

"Then stop judging my mother. It's not your business."

He raised an eyebrow. "You made it my business."

She peeked at him. She couldn't even believe him right now. He didn't know her mother, yet he judged her so badly.

All this was her father's fault. He didn't tell them the truth about the matter—all he told them was her mother abandoned her.

"Stop the car!" she said.

Matthias's brow creased with worry. "What? I should stop the car? Why?"

"Stop the car, Matthias. I want to get down." She hit her palm on the door.

He shook his head. "We haven't reached the destination yet. Your mother surely doesn't live in the trees."

She glared at him, choosing her words carefully. "Let me get down, or I swear, I will jump out of this moving car. That would be on you."

This got to him as he quickly parked to the other side of the road.

"What is wrong, Iyawa? Do I need to remind you we are in the middle of nowhere?"

"You should be going back to the hotel and enjoy your vacation. If you are going to help me out of pity, I don't want it." She reached for the door.

He held her arm. "What? I am not helping you out of pity. I am helping you as a friend."

She paused, placed a hand on his, and jerked it away. "We are not friends, Matthias. Nothing close to friends. This whole thing is giving ideas I don't like."

But before she could even open the door, a knock at the driver's seat window grabbed their attention. There was a loud bang bang, and it continued.

She shifted back in her seat as panic swelled up inside her. There were people in this street? This place seemed like a jungle.

A shadowy figure dressed in a black outfit and face covered with a mask appeared with something that looked like a gun, and Iyawa could tell the gun did look bloodthirsty.

"Oh, no!" Matthias cursed, his eyes widening with terror.

The man was now thumping heavily on the window.

"Matthias, lock all the doors," she shouted.

Before he could do the right thing, the man had opened the door and now had the gun pointed at him. Jesus, that was truly a gun.

Chapter Ten

What should one do in a situation like this? Perhaps drive away from the scene, but this man was holding a gun, and he had opened the door. Was she going to die before she saw her mother?

"Get out!" the man shouted. "Get out of the car, or I blow your head."

"Matthias. Why wouldn't you even lock the car?" she said.

Matthias's expression grew still. "Can we stop passing blame now? I mean, right in front of danger."

Iyawa gulped down a series of breaths to stay quiet. Her legs suddenly grew weak as she managed to get down from the vehicle.

Matthias raised his hands in surrender as the man roughly dragged him away from the car.

The man glanced at Iyawa on the other side and urged her to move close. "Drop everything you have. Your money, pieces of jewellery, and purse. Everything."

Matthias hurriedly removed his golden wristwatch and chain and handed it over to the man.

"What are you doing? Take off your jewellery." The robber approached her, placing the gun to her head. "Do you want me to shoot you here, right now? I might be caught after this, but that won't wake up your already dead body."

"Let her be. Please, do not hurt her," Matthias pleaded.

Iyawa removed her silver earrings and chain and handed it over to him. "Here, have them."

The robber turned to Matthias. "The keys of this car. Give them to me right now."

Matthias took a step back. "Please take everything but not this car. It is not mine. It's for a friend."

The robber used the bottom of the gun to hit him across the face. Iyawa whimpered. This guy was hitting Matthias, and it was all her fault. Matthias shifted back and touched the corner of his lips, viewing the red liquid smudged on his finger.

"Please, you need to understand. I would give you the car if it was for me. I am not the owner," he pleaded.

The sight of his bruised lips made Iyawa's blood boil. Why was he pleading with a thief? Rari was supposed to be understanding if this was what Matthias was concerned about.

"You are a bastard," the robber yelled.

Matthias rubbed off the blood on his lips, but the man wasn't done. He lunged at Matthias and kicked him with his knee in his stomach a few times.

Matthias coughed out, holding his stomach. He placed his hand on the car for support.

"Give me the key now," the robber said, his hand stretched forth.

"Give him the keys, Matthias. Are you insane?" she yelled.

Immediately, Matthias handed over the key to the robber. The man eyed the key with a mischievous glint in his eyes and placed it in his pocket, making a move towards Matthias.

No, you don't. Iyawa checked around with her eyes. She bent over to grab a long metal rod.

Before the robber turned took at her, she lifted the rod and hit it hard on his head. The robber held his hand to his head in pain, and Iyawa used that opportunity to grab Matthias by the hand.

The robber cocked his gun and shot at them, but she had already fled into the bush with Matthias. The bullet only missed her by a tree. It seemed like the robber didn't follow them into the bush, and she could hear the distant sound of a car zooming off.

God, they were doomed. The robber had gone with the car, and they were in the bush with no money and phone.

Matthias coughed. He leaned against a big tree for support, hands still clutching his stomach.

She placed a hand on his back and suddenly became conscious of her shaking hand.

"Matthias, are you okay? You know, you could have just given him the keys without being hurt. Why did you let it escalate?"

When he didn't respond, she shook his arm lightly. "Matthias, I am talking to you. You could have gotten us killed."

He groaned, his voice also sharp. "No, you would have gotten us killed if you didn't have to make a huge scene. I was a fool to have stopped the car."

"Do not blame this on me. You were the one talking about my mother in a way I didn't like."

"What way, Iyawa? I apologized, and still, you wanted me to stop the car. You are such a drama queen," he hissed.

His eyes were distant and icy, and for a moment, she was afraid of him.

"Then why did you stop? You could have ignored me and continue driving, you know?" she said, keenly aware of his scrutiny.

Why was he passing blame right now?

He sighed. "Because you asked me to."

Something tugged at her heart. Iyawa knew deep down he was right. This was her fault. If she had not forced him to stop the car, they would have been on their way to her mother's place.

She gave a low, long sigh as she avoided his gaze. "Matthias, I am sorry. I didn't know we were going to get robbed and, I...I was just so angry at you."

"Look, I just want you to know I came here to help you of my own free will. And I will never judge your mother because I don't know anything about her. I am sorry if I made you feel the way." His expression softened.

"I know. I...overreacted and got you hurt for no reason. I am such a terrible person."

"Ah, Iyawa finally has a heart?" The glint of humour had returned to his face.

She rolled her eyes. "I will take it you aren't hurt anymore. If that is so, let us find a way to get out of this place. It is giving me the creeps."

"Oh, no, where is this place?" Matthias took a glance around the forest.

Iyawa inhaled the minty smell and continued on, not ignoring the sound of her feet sliding through the leaves.

"It is just a forest, Matthias. We can find our way around here."

He scoffed. "First, we don't know where we are, so I don't think we should just keep walking. We are in a forest. It's dangerous."

She halted, placing her hands on her hip. She knew right now wouldn't be the best time to start an argument, but he needed to understand her. "We can't just stay here and expect good Samaritans to come out of nowhere. We need to get out of this forest, and the first thing is by finding the route we took down here."

Matthias sighed and rubbed his forehead. "Im, for crying out loud, how is that even possible? You do not even remember how we came in. Look around, this forest is thick. We would get lost."

The rustling sounds of small animals scurrying under the thick ferns snapped at her attention. The breeze swayed gently, and birds could be seen flying from tree to tree.

"We just sit down and do nothing? Jeez, we don't even have our phones, so no GPS. We are stuck here. Stuck with no phone or anything to call for help."

"Erm…I think the address won't be a problem. I still have it on a paper here in case anyone comes to help." Matthias's smile was boyishly affectionate.

But Iyawa was in no mood for it.

Roughly, she thrust herself away from him. "Yes, and I have it up in my head. Matthias, I have been waiting for this all my life, remember. We have to keep walking, please."

His brows flickered a little. "Why must everything about you come with an argument? You do always think you are right."

"That is not true. I am just trying to be reasonable here."

"By suggesting we go deeper into a forest we have no idea what's in it and get lost with no one to help us?" He walked forward and stopped in front of her.

"Do you have any other idea, Matthias? Or we just rely on your hope?"

He drew his lips together thoughtfully. "You won't take no for an answer, anyways. Let's just try your idea, and if it doesn't work, we are doomed."

She waved him dismissively. "Stop whining like a baby."

.. ∽∞ ..

AFTER WALKING FOR WHAT seemed like an hour, Iyawa and Matthias realized they were now deeper into the forest with no beginning or end.

She gave a mental groan. Matthias was going to haunt her for this. This forest was really thick.

She was so caught in her thoughts, she didn't notice a small rock in front of her, and it wasn't until she had tripped on it did she realize it was there.

"Are you okay?" Matthias asked.

She winced and touched her leg, not failing to send a glare in his direction. "Yes! Of course I am okay. I just hit my leg on a rock, and it's refreshing."

He offered her a forgiving smile that melted a part of her. Even in his dishevelled state, he looked like a piece of candy.

"I am sorry. Can you walk?"

"Can we take a rest here, please? I am feeling so weak already."

He straightened, sighing loudly. "I was thinking about that, too. This journey doesn't seem like it is going to end."

She tried to stand up, but he stopped her.

"Hey, what are you—"

He reached out and swung her up, bridal style. Iyawa was abruptly motionless for long seconds.

He stared at her for a moment, his dark eyes serenely compelling. "Do you have any problem with this?"

"Can we just go? This is awkward."

He gave a nervous smile and inspected the forest before walking farther into it.

As he inched closer, Iyawa could see clear pathways on the floor. Finally! A route that might lead to modernization.

"Look. Over there!" Matthias said.

In the distance, she could see a small barn at the other side of the forest. It seemed desolate as some of the wooden roof had gone rough with wear. By now, they'd been walking for so long, and the setting sun had given a warm orange tinge to the sky.

When they arrived at the barn, Matthias dropped Iyawa to the ground, and she managed to stand. They both stood in front of the barn, giving it a thorough look. It was like they were both weighing the idea of staying the night here.

"This is it. We will stay here for the night," he announced.

She squinted her gaze. "Huh?"

"Don't turn this into an argument, please? We have no other option."

"You have got to be kidding me. This barn looks like it hasn't been used for years. Are you telling me we are staying here?"

He looked at her. "I am telling you you have no choice. If you still want to find your mother by tomorrow morning, we stay here for the night."

"We could find somewhere better in front." She ignored his commanding tone.

Matthias scoffed. "You should not be talking about walking farther into that forest. It is because of you we are now lost with no sign of hope."

"I was expecting you to blame me for this. You always do." She sighed dramatically.

Iyawa folded her arms and watched him walk up to the front door of the barn. Beside the door was a wooden chair, and she guessed an older person had been living there.

"Look, everything is fine. What are you even scared of, anyway? I thought nothing scared you."

"Nothing scares me, Matthias."

He chuckled and moved to sit in the wooden chair. "Your father scares me. You have that look—"

Before he could finish his sentence, the chair gave way to rot, and his rear end hit the ground. He rose to his feet, his face contoured in pain as he rubbed his backside in circular motions.

"God, that was not what I expected of this chair."

Iyawa shook her head in slight amusement. "Please tell me our fake engagement was not for better or worse. Because you are so embarrassing."

Matthias gave her a look that sent her laughing.

Time passed away quickly, and the clouds were already dark. Iyawa had gone with him to gather twigs and branches, and they'd made a fireplace in front of the barn. With some extra searching, they were able to find ripe blackberries for the night.

She rubbed her hands together and stretched them in front of the firewood. It was a small fire, but it still managed to lighten up the environment.

She looked at Matthias. He was still throwing blackberries into his mouth.

"I don't think you know, and I know it doesn't concern you, but I am scared of the dark. That's why I suggested we make a big wood fire," Matthias said, not removing his gaze from the fire.

She glanced at him. "I…I….Erm…I don't know what to say. You should have told me back when we were picking sticks."

"You had a point back when you said a bigger fire might cause unwanted attraction. Who knows what lives behind those trees?"

She feigned annoyance. "Dude."

"Sorry. I am just bored. Not used to just sitting around." He chuckled, popping another berry into his mouth.

"Me, too."

"Hey, can we just ask random questions and one will answer? You know, to kill off time."

She raised an eyebrow. "Okay? What questions?"

"Tell me about your family."

Her stomach twitched. "There is no much to know, if that's what you are wondering. We are just the Jaseth family."

"Come on. Just describe them to me."

Iyawa opened her mouth, but he stopped her.

"Don't forget to introduce yourself, please."

She frowned. "Don't test my patience."

He urged her on with a wave on his hand.

"I am Iyawa Jaseth from the Jaseth family. We are a family of three. We were four before Jadesola's mom, Aunt Madeline, died of cancer. So it's just Popsi, Jadesola, and me."

"Yeah, Jadesola's mom. That's so sad. Father told me your dad was greatly affected by her death."

She shrugged, recollecting how he tried to stay strong by burying himself in his business. "Yeah. He couldn't get over the fact she was gone. Sometimes, I thought he wouldn't be able to get over it."

Years after Jadesola's mom died, he called her name sometimes by mistake, and whenever he realized she wasn't there to answer him, he would break down in tears. Perhaps it was safe to say her death had had a hand in his personality now.

"Hmm, I'm sorry to hear this. Death really changes people in a way."

She swallowed. "Don't be. Tell me about yours."

"My name is Matthias. I'm thirty-three years old, and I'm from Nigeria. My family is a family of three, too, now as my sister is married, so it's safe to say her husband and child are part of our family. We've always been a small family, but we still thrived to be closer. We would have meals together and do lots of fun things."

She smiled at him. "You are so lucky."

Iyawa felt an odd twinge of guilt. Here was this man helping her find her mother out here in the forest, and she couldn't even tell him the whole truth about her life. It was a topic she didn't want to open for now. Things were changing, but she didn't want to access them yet.

"Matthias."

He reduced the intensity of his chewing. "Yes?"

She sighed, steepled her fingers together, and stared at them. "I...I want to ask a question, and I need you to be honest with me."

His eyebrows raised a fraction. "Okay?"

"What do you truly know about my mother? Do not lie to me."

"I have told you, Iyawa. All I know is what your father told my dad and me. He said your mother didn't want you, and he took you away."

"Well, he lied. I don't know, but I don't just believe him, Matthias. My mom and I were friends. She loved me. There was no reason for her to just leave me."

He wiped his mouth with his palm. "And I believe every word you say. It's not for me to judge you."

She nodded back at him without speaking for a while.

"Im, is there something on your mind?"

She sighed. A long, deep one.

"There is a reason why no one knows my mother."

"What do you mean?"

"My... mother, Matthias. She...is just a one-night-stand with my dad." She buried her face in her palms.

"So I've heard. Is that why your dad is so embarrassed to talk about her?"

"My father thinks she was an obstacle to his marriage. He was guilty. I'm sure he wanted to save face in public, so he snatched me from her."

She watched him with keenly observant eyes, the flames illuminating the emotion plastered on his features.

He blinked. "You think that's what happened? He feels guilty?"

She nodded. "Yes. Maybe you didn't realize, but he really loved his wife. Why he cheated on her, I don't know. He didn't even know my mom 'til the fateful day."

Matthias opened his mouth to say something but closed it.

"I know you have something to say, so just spare us all the time and say it."

"Im, I didn't—"

"Don't sugarcoat it, Matthias. You want to think you know why I'm like this, but I am sorry, I have no answers. I grew up meeting this confused family." She felt a shudder of humiliation.

Matthias's lips parted. "Calm down, Iyawa. Just relax and listen to me."

She looked at him.

His eyes widened with concern. "I am not going to judge anyone, I told you. Look, she is your mother, and one thing I know about mothers is they always have a reason for doing things."

Why was he always calm? She never talked about her mother. Why was he different? She was feeling all sorts of emotions right now, and the anxiety in her had run a thousand miles.

"This is why I always hate confession time," she murmured to herself.

He exhaled. "Relax. I don't even know your mother, Iyawa. I only know you."

"Yeah. I did bad things, Matthias. Why do you even care?"

"You said it yourself, you've changed. I sincerely do care about only you. I don't know why."

She whipped her head so fast, she thought she heard a bone crack. Even if it was a husky whisper, she knew she'd heard him right. Did he truly care for her? Did she hear him right?

Iyawa stared wordlessly across at him, her heart pounding. Matthias was a gentleman, and she was sure he said this to all his friends. There was absolutely no meaning to it.

She was never told only she mattered, and it was sweet hearing it from him.

"We will find your mother tomorrow, I promise. Right now, we need to rest."

She nodded, unable to form words.

Matthias rose from his position on the ground and dusted his hands. "You should come in now. You can't be out here all by yourself."

"I will be right inside," she told him. "You go on."

He gave her a charming smile before entering the barn.

What just happened?

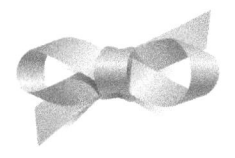

Chapter Eleven

When Iyawa woke up the next morning, she found herself in the dark, looming barn again. Last night, she had slept on a plank while Matthias slept on the floor. She didn't expect to find a piece of clothing comforting her body this morning. It was Mattias's black shirt he had been wearing last night.

She rubbed the sleep off her eyes and scanned the barn again. There was no sign of Matthias in the room. Just his shirt.

She jolted upright from the plank and called out for him. There was no reply. Standing and making her way outside, she tried not to touch the dirty windows and doors.

Outside, there was still no sign of him.

"Matthias," she called again.

Where did he go without telling her? He wouldn't possibly leave her all by herself, right?

She kept walking forward and stopped when she heard a splash of water behind some shrubs.

When she opened the shrubs, she could see a pair of shoes discarded on the floor.

Emerging from underneath the water was Matthias, fully clothed. Rubbing the water off his face, he gasped for air.

Before she could react or say anything, a green, creepy insect flew in and perched on her arm. She swallowed, trying to stay calm.

It was just an insect looking *sickly*. It had a horrible face, and she began swatting it away silently lest she give way to her hiding place.

"Yikes! Get off me, you stupid insect." She wiped her arm so much, one would think she would tear it apart from her shoulder.

"Iyawa?" Matthias turned to look at her. He went lower into the water, the surface revealing just his head.

Intense colouring touched her face. "Erm...I am sorry. I...I didn't know you were there. Why are you even out here?"

"I came here to take a bath. I was reeking of yesterday's sweat, and it was nauseating. This way, I'm also washing my outfit. You were looking for me, weren't you?" Matthias smiled amusingly, possibly at her rush of words.

"Wouldn't you do the same if you woke up in a strange place and couldn't find the other?"

"Sorry. You were deep in your sleep, and I couldn't disturb you. Can I tell you now you have an adorable snore?"

She threw back her head and placed her hands on her hips. "I do not know what you are talking about. Just because I heard you snore doesn't give you the right to lie."

"I know, but you did snore. I just felt it was annoying."

"I do not snore."

"Yes, you do. You were like this." He demonstrated. "And I was like, this woman is something else when she is asleep."

She rolled her eyes. "Just shut up, Matthias. Get out of the water, and let us continue our journey."

He shook his head and rolled his fingers on the surface of the water. "I'm almost done. Hey, why don't you also take a bath? Trust me, you need a bath."

She folded her arms across her chest. "Are you saying I smell?"

"No. I am saying you need a bath. Yesterday's stress is going to leave you all dirty and unappealing."

She looked at the water. "Only heaven knows what has been in that water. I can't step into it."

"It is just water, Iyawa. God, you are such a neat freak."

When Matthias left the water and waited for his clothes to dry, they began their journey, walking down a straight line.

"You know, you've never told me about your ex."

He turned to look at her. "Oh, there is nothing to talk about."

"Why did you two break up?"

"Iyawa, if you think our breakup came with hard feelings, it didn't. We still do hang out together."

Her stomach hardened. "Huh? You still do meet up with her? Why?"

"We... Our breakup was pretty mutual." He gave a single shoulder shrug that broke easily.

"Really? The first time I brought up her name, it didn't look so mutual."

"I said it was mutual."

She poked a finger at him. "No, it isn't. You are a liar."

"Okay, fine. I will tell you."

"Well, talk."

"She broke up with me."

She scoffed. "That's a fact as old as time."

She didn't know why it mattered to her, but knowing Matthias still kept in touch with his ex who had broken up with him sent a burning sensation through her.

"Why did she break up with you?"

He sighed and looked at her. "She said I was boring."

"Boring? She broke up with you because she thought you were boring?"

He nodded. "Weeks after the breakup, I couldn't move on with my life. I mean, what does she mean by boring?"

Iyawa knew Matthias wasn't boring. He was sweet even if she couldn't admit this to him. He had this outgoing nature that seemed to brighten a room. It was why she couldn't take her eyes off him all those years ago.

Her face reddened. "I don't want to say this, but your girlfriend was cheating on you. That you are boring is just for you to blame yourself."

He halted in his strides. "What? I gave her all my love, and she did this to me? I knew something was not right. I am not a boring man."

"Yeah, you are not. Is your girlfriend really pretty?"

"Ex, Iyawa, and yes, she is pretty. Why?"

She snapped her fingers. "Ahah. Pretty girls are like devils. They'll break your heart. You'll get over it."

"Not all pretty girls." He gave her a warm smile. "I am looking at one."

Iyawa's tongue tangled. She could not believe her ears. Clearly, he was playing games. *Look at that smile,* she told herself.

Just then, they heard a distant sound. It seemed like a vehicle zooming off.

Matthias widened his eyes. "Is that what I think it is?"

"It is a car. Finally, sound of civilization."

He pointed to the other end of the forest. "I think it is coming from that side. Never thought I would be so happy to hear a car."

As they ran down the forest, Iyawa felt her left hand being pulled gently. She tried to ignore the fluttering feeling as they made their way past trees and branches.

Finally, they made it to the other side of the forest, and as they came out of the thick bush, she came across a tarmac path separating her from going over to the other end.

Matthias swat his fist in the air. "Yes. We made it. We made it out of the forest."

"All we have to do is get a car. We don't even know what side of South Africa we are in right now."

"Trust me, it is not going to be that easy. No one wants to help two strangers in the middle of the forest," he pointed.

And he was right. Thirty minutes had passed, and yet, no one slowed down to render help.

"Are all humans like this?" She groaned. "What did God say about helping your neighbours?"

Matthias shrugged. "Some won't help because of security risk. While some wouldn't help because we don't really look like we need help."

Iyawa thought on it for a while. "Do I have to be pregnant or weak or bruised before they render help? Can't anyone just help us now?"

"It is just the way things are, babe."

She scoffed. "I would get a cab now. Just watch and learn."

He chuckled. "No one is going to help you out here, Iyawa."

She waved down a Jeep, but the vehicle didn't even slow down. It just zoomed off.

"I can see how good you are doing to get us a cab," he said.

There was a black vehicle coming, and Iyawa waved it down. To her surprise, it stopped.

Thankfully, the man was a good Samaritan who offered to take them to their destination.

"Thank you so much," Matthias said to him, closing the car door after Iyawa.

The good Samaritan zoomed off, and soon, they even reached their destination.

Iyawa looked at the street matching the name on the paper in her hand. As they walked into it, looking out for the number where her mother was located, they soon stopped a building.

Matthias peeked at the paper in her hand. "Are you sure this is the right building?"

She nodded. "It should be."

Iyawa sized up the small bungalow with beautiful flowers surrounding the compound. It looked like a place where any normal family would stay.

"It is so silent, you could guess no one is home." His brows arched up. "What do we do now?"

"Go in and tell my mother I am her long-lost daughter. That is if she even remembers me."

Matthias stopped her. "No matter what, do not yell at your mother. Calm down, and let her explain everything to you, okay?"

"Okay, Matthias. Can we go now?"

All she needed was a nod of approval, but he surprised her by holding her hand as they entered the garden and walked to the front door. For a moment, she felt a hint of spirited security. It was like Matthias was telling her they were in this together.

When they got to the red door, Iyawa could feel every second pass as she stared at the panel. Was she finally going to see her mother? What if her mother didn't recognize her anymore?

Matthias's hold on her hand tightened some more. Iyawa knocked on the door. She held her breath until the door was opened by a young girl who looked like she was in her teenage years. She was wearing an apron.

This must be her sister. Iyawa couldn't help but feel jealous. Her smile was so wide, one could tell she had never known what suffering meant. Her skin was brown and beautiful, her brown eyes staring back at Iyawa.

"Good evening," Matthias said.

It was then she realized she had been staring at the girl for a while now.

"Good evening. Who are you?" the girl asked.

"I...erm...We...I..." Iyawa shuddered inwardly at her lack of words. She had planned to see her mother's family, and now, she was embarrassing herself. Maybe she wasn't ready for this. This was all wrong. Coming here unannounced to visit someone who might not even remember her?

Just then, a voice behind the girl made her look up.

"Nandi, what did I tell you about opening the door for strangers? Who is there?"

"It's a woman and a man," Nandi replied.

There was this heavy feeling in her stomach as she stared back at her mother. Yes, it was her own mother. Also wearing a yellow apron with the drawing of a cartoon character. The older woman has changed since the last time Iyawa had seen her. Her skin wasn't as brown as it used to be—it now had a lighter shade. She could still see the resemblance between them even if no one did.

"Get inside, Nandi. Go take a look at your brother. He must be messing up that cake." The older woman turned to them. "Good evening. How may I help you?"

"Are you Tito?" Iyawa asked.

Her mother hesitated at her words and blinked in a dazed expression. She closed the door behind her, turning to look at them. "How did you know this name? No one here knows this name. Who are you guys?"

"You are Tito?" Iyawa asked.

Her mother stared at her for a moment like she was weighing her answer. "Yes."

Iyawa felt a little tugging at her chest. "Then you must know me, Mom."

This time, Matthias placed a hand on her shoulder. How should she have broken it to her mother that she was her long-lost daughter? The woman didn't even recognize her.

"Mom? I am not your— Wait, Im...Iyawa? Is that really you?" Her mother slapped a hand over her mouth. "You are Iyawa? My...my daughter?"

"You remember me? Mom, you remember me. You know my name." Iyawa knew she sounded ridiculous at the moment.

Her mother brushed Iyawa's cheeks with her palm before giving her a big hug. "Why wouldn't I remember your name? You are my daughter. You've grown so well, I can't even recognize you. What are you doing in SA? You shouldn't be here."

Iyawa broke from the hug to look at the older woman. "Why? Mom, I have missed you."

Her mother's eyes were glassy with tears, and Iyawa was sure she was about to say something before a voice interrupted her.

"Maria," a chubby man called. He looked like he was in his mid-fifties, and he was holding grocery bags like he could use some help.

Who is Maria? Iyawa wanted to ask. It wasn't until her mother walked down the porch steps to help the man with the bags that she got a hint of who Maria was.

The man placed a quick kiss on her mother's lips and turned to Iyawa with a curious smile. It seemed genuine, so even she couldn't get angry at him.

"Maria, you didn't tell me you were expecting a visitor. Good evening."

Only Matthias returned the greeting. Iyawa didn't even know what to say.

"Oh, I didn't know they were also visiting. Iyawa here is a relative of mine, and she came to see me. It's been a long time since I've seen her," her mother said.

The impact of her mother's words sent a shockwave down her body. A relative? She knew this man was her mother's husband, so why was her mother denying her?

"A relative? Maria, this is good news." The man turned to them as he approached. "I have never seen a relative of Maria's before. She claims she doesn't keep in contact with any of them. Thanks for reaching out, Iyawa. Is this your...?"

Matthias nodded. "Yes. I am Iyawa's fiancé. Nice to meet you."

"I hope you two are staying the night? We would like for you to spend the night with us. Besides, you should really taste the food Nandi has prepared tonight with her mother."

Maria shook her head. "David, I am sure Iyawa and her fiancé have other plans. They just stopped by to check up on me. Right?"

Iyawa looked at Matthias—the disappointment on her face must be obvious to him. Why was her mother so keen on sending her away?

"Actually, we have no means of getting back tonight, so we wouldn't mind staying over. What do you think, dear?"

Matthias smiled. "I think that would be just great."

She'd just met her mother, and she wasn't going to just go like that. She needed answers, and her mother was going to give them to her.

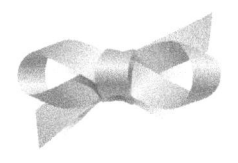

Chapter Twelve

Iyawa knew her mother was living well. From the soft cushion covers and beautiful throws with the brown wool rug to the colourful crayon scribbles on the brown wall, she could tell her mother was living her best life. Right now, she was seated on one of those cushions with David and Matthias while her mother and Nandi were nowhere to be found.

It seemed David noticed her staring at the walls because he called on a young boy who hugged him. "Pardon the walls, Iyawa. Junior has a habit of scribbling on them."

She was about to wave away his concerns when Matthias piped up.

"That is bound to happen in a place where kids are. When I was little, my younger sister had a habit of doing this. It took God's grace to stop her."

The men burst into laughter while Iyawa could only look on. Her nannies wouldn't let her litter her toys, let alone scribbling on the walls. She couldn't blame them. They were working for her father. Even Jadesola wasn't allowed to scribble on the walls.

When her mother came out later, it was to call everyone to the dining table.

This was supposed to be me setting the table with my mama.

The table itself looked like it was hosting a feast. White rice served with a sauce, which Nandi made sure to call Tomato

Bredie. When they all took their seats and started eating, Iyawa couldn't stop playing with her spoon. She hadn't come here to eat. She'd come here to find her mother. Said mother whose attention was taken by Junior who couldn't stop being messy with his food.

"Iyawa, are you okay?" Matthias whispered.

She looked at his plate. He also hadn't eaten much.

"I am fine. Why did you ask?"

He peered at her plate. "You haven't taken a spoon of your rice. Why, you are not hungry?"

"Look who is talking. See your plate. I am just not hungry."

"So, Iyawa. How are you related to Mama?" Nandi asked, scooping a spoon of rice into her mouth. "Are you her younger sister or something?"

Iyawa shifted her gaze to her mother who looked at her in panic.

What is she so scared of?

"Aunt Iyawa, Nandi. What did I tell you about talking while eating?" her mother scolded.

Nandi rolled her eyes. "Mama, it was just a question. I am not a baby anymore."

David chuckled, using his hand to pat his daughter's head. "Yes, yes. You are sixteen now. We know. Maria, there is no harm in asking. Today is a happy day. We finally met one of your relatives."

"It is fine, really. I am—"

"She is my aunt's daughter."

Iyawa didn't know when her spoon escaped from her grip. "What?"

Matthias held her hand. "It is fine, Iyawa."

"Oh, really? I didn't know you had an aunt. That's so good." David was really believing her mother's lies.

Her mother was avoiding her gaze, and Iyawa didn't know what annoyed her more. Maybe the fact her own mother didn't want her new family to know about her, or that her mother couldn't even spare her a look.

"Of course, I had an aunt. She died years back. Iyawa just dropped by to say hi."

"Oh, I am sorry about your loss, Iyawa," David said.

Iyawa could only nod. After all, it was the only response to a situation like this.

"Well, when the kids are in school tomorrow, you could take Iyawa and Matthias out and have some fun together. I have a long day with the men tomorrow," David told her mother.

This time, her mother looked at her with a smile. "Oh, David, that is so good. That would be great."

· · ⚘ · ·

IYAWA'S MOTHER OPENED the door to the guest room, not trying to hide her smile. Iyawa glanced around once she was in. The room was small, with cream-colored walls. Two small beds sat in the middle, with a chair and table in one corner. Aside from this, it was empty. Even the smell was a musty one. It was evident no one had been here in a long time.

Her mother shook her head. "We rarely have visitors. Sorry about the room."

"You think I am concerned about the room? What was that about? You lied, Mom." Iyawa folded her arms, giving her mother a disappointed look.

"Does David know about Iyawa?" Matthias asked.

Her mother shut the door closed after looking through the hallway. She ran a hand over her head and let out a sigh. "My daughter, I really apologize. I can't explain things now, but we will talk tomorrow."

"I don't understand why you did that."

Her mother cupped her left cheek. "I wish I could explain now, but I can't. We'll talk tomorrow."

And with that, she left.

Matthias cleared his throat.

Iyawa turned to look at him. "What? If you have something to say, just say it."

"I just don't want you to overthink things. Whatever happened now shouldn't stress you so much. Your mother must have an explanation."

All the hidden anger from the dinner came back swimming through her body.

"Overthink things? Matthias, what just happened there?"

"I don't know. Unless you have a talk with your mother, I don't want you jumping to conclusions."

"My mother is denying me, Matthias."

Saying it now made it feel real. Her mother was denying her, and it felt heart-breaking somehow. And as she slept during the night, different thoughts ran through her mind.

· · ❧ · ·

THE NEXT MORNING CAME so fast. A knock on the door woke Iyawa up. It was her mother.

Matthias offered to drive them to a local restaurant. According to her mother, the house was clear. The kids—her half-siblings—were at school while David was at work. When they got to the open restaurant, Matthias stayed back in the car. She tried looking at him from the rear mirror, but all he did was look out the window, his gaze focused on the pink flowers surrounding the restaurant.

"Why don't you come with us, Matthias?" she asked him.

Her mother bent down to look at him through the window. "Yes. Won't you be bored sitting here all alone?"

He didn't look at them. "I will rather not disturb the reunion. Besides, I can put on the radio to distract me."

They went in, leaving him outside.

Her mother's hand on her clenched fist startled Iyawa out of her thoughts.

"You sure you okay? You've been staring at your food for like...let me see...five minutes."

Sitting in front of her mom, watching as her mother shoved a spoon full of an orangey stuff and rice into her mouth, she wondered if she should bring up the issue of her ignoring her the day before.

"Sorry. I...I was just staring at the food. I have never eaten this before."

Her mother chuckled. "Of course you haven't. It is called Chakalaka. Come on, take a bite."

She took a spoon and cupped it into her mouth. "Chakalaka is quite spicy. It is good."

"I know, right. Try it with bread, and you would see how delicious it is. The foods in SA here are wonderful. I cook these dishes myself."

Iyawa offered a bemused smile. "I remember when you still allowed me do pretend cooking back in that big kitchen."

"Oh, I am sorry. I don't even remember." Her mother gave a long pause, making her heart pound. "Do you even know how to cook now? It has been a difficult thing for you to learn since you were a kid. That, I still remember."

She took a deep intake of breath. "Yeah. I just don't think it is something I like. But as it is, I have no choice. My mother-in-law-to-be requires me to cook."

"Nigerians. Are we ever going to let women live their lives? Thank God, that boy loves you."

"He doesn't love me."

"Coming here to help you find your mother and waiting in the car while you chit-chat with her? That is something only someone in love will do. And I see the way you look at him." Her mother gave a slow smile, her head cocked to the side.

Iyawa made a noise in her throat. "No, I don't look at him in any way."

She didn't realize there was a way she looked at Matthias. Besides, she was not into him that way. He was just a friend.

"Yes, you do. You couldn't stop looking at him on our way here. He is a cute one, you know?"

"Mom. Stop." She shuffled her feet under the table. "How can you even tell if I love someone?"

Her mother dropped her spoon and leaned back in her seat, chest out. "I know how it feels to love someone. Look at David and me."

Iyawa gave a slow shake of the head. "Yes, I see you love him so much."

"Yes."

"How did you know you were in love?"

Her mother's shoulders lifted in a loose manner. "You just feel it. It's something only you can confirm."

"Then I am not in love with him because I can't feel anything."

Her mother looked at her with pity. "You are just like me. I was scared, too. Your grandparents had a terrible married life. It was so irritating the way their love life went down the hill. I didn't want something like that, but now, look at me."

Her eyebrows furrowed at the word grandparents. She had never been associated with those words. It all felt strange. Suddenly, she wanted to know more.

"Who are they?"

"Who?"

"My grandparents. Tell me about my grandparents."

The older woman cleared her throat. "Ah. They are both Nigerians, and both illiterates."

Iyawa had heard of such people from way back when. Some didn't go to school while those that did were mostly men. Back then, everyone believed a woman's place was in the kitchen.

"Your grandparents. They were so in love. But back in those days, men had to marry more than one wife. You know, so they can reproduce more so more kids can help on farm."

"Then what happened to them?" she asked.

"My mother was rather betrayed. She felt it was because she couldn't reproduce more. I was her only child, but she never paid attention to me. She just wanted to have more kids. One day, she grew sick and died." Her mother cleared her throat like she didn't want to remember such. "My stepmothers mistreated me, and my father didn't care. So I ran away. I grew up fending for myself."

Iyawa placed a hand on her mother's. "I am sorry, Ma."

"Sorry? I am not sad. It just hurts to know my father didn't really care about my mother or me." She gave a scoff. "I am good, baby. You are lucky, you know. Matthew or whatever you call him, that guy, he loves you. Keep him."

"He doesn't, ma." Her mother had been honest with her, and she wasn't going to keep lying to her.

"What? Aren't you going to get married? If he doesn't love you, why are you marrying him?"

Iyawa glimpsed at the door of the restaurant. "We are not really a real couple."

They were done eating now, and her mother waited for the waiter to clear up the plates. "What? Then...then why are you wearing a ring?"

"It was a plan by Popsi to save my reputation. People in Nigeria respect him a lot, and my actions were going to ruin our chances of selling very high." She glanced at her fingers. Saying the words out made her sound like a spoilt teenager. Was this how people viewed her?

Her mother's mouth was slightly open. "You call him Popsi?"

"Oh. It is a thing my sister and I call him. When we were little—"

"Your sister? You have a sister?"

Iyawa's lips curled. If it had been someone else, she would think the fellow was trying to call Jadesola her half-sister. "She is my sister, ma. I know we are half-sister, but Jadesola is even more than a sister to me. She is...like my soulmate."

"Oh, is that so? What does her mother have to say about it? Does she even see you as her own child?"

Iyawa's neck shrunk as she looked at her mom. "Jeez, Mom. She is dead. Aunt Madeline was the best stepmother to me before she died. She didn't treat me differently."

"That's good. You have a good relationship with your father's family. This is great news."

Iyawa's eyebrows were raised. Why was her mother so happy?

Her Aunt Madeline had been the best to her, and it pained her she wasn't there to see her and Jadesola grow to become the women she might have wanted.

Her mother gave a long sigh. "Tell me about your reputation instead. Why does it need saving?"

"Nothing much. I...I have this habit of doing bad stuff when I am in distress."

"So? Don't we all?"

"It is kind of different, ma. It is—"

"What? The worst thing you could be doing is to murder someone. Even God forgives us for our sins."

Iyawa was silent for a while. She then remembered what she had wanted to ask her mother.

"Mom, have you ever thought of me while I was with Popsi? Do you even remember me?"

"Iyawa—"

Matthias's words came rushing in her mind. "If you really cared for me, you would have searched for me."

"Search for you? Why would I search for you when I know where you were?" Her mother looked at her in confusion.

Iyawa leaned away from the table. "What do you mean?"

"I knew you were with your father. I dropped you with him."

That was all it took for her life to shatter. She remained motionless on her seat. "Wh...what? B...but Dad took me away from you."

Her mother's brow furrowed. "No. He didn't. You see, your father was very supportive. Even after your birth strained his relationship with his wife, he would give me anything I asked for."

"No, Mom. That's not true."

"I don't know what your father told you, but I had to drop you with him. I couldn't drop you with my family. They hated me for having a child with a man I didn't know. I was young then. I made mistakes."

Iyawa felt the screams of frustration at the back of her throat. "I don't understand. Why did you drop me?"

Her mother reached for her hand. "I am sorry, Iyawa. I didn't want a child. I had my whole life in front of me. You...you were a distraction. But you had a loving father who wanted you. There was nothing I could do. His wife met me one day and promised me she was going to take care of you. She was a nice woman, you see."

"You didn't want me?"

"Iyawa, you have to understand. I was young."

Swallowing back sobs, she looked at her mother. "What about now? You can't tell David I am your child."

"Because you are in my past. David doesn't need to know. He...he would think I lied about myself. I just want to be happy with my family. If you understand what I mean. That doesn't mean I don't love you. I do."

She flung out her hands in despair. "I am also your child. I don't deserve to be hidden like that. I just want to get to know you more. Do you know how hard I tried to feel among my mates? I've messed up my life thinking it's because you were absent in my life, and you don't even want me?"

"What happened between your father and me was a mistake. Go to your father, Iyawa. I'm always your mother. I do love you. I'll get you money to go back home, but you can't stay here too long. David will be suspicious."

Mistake. That word again.

Why does everybody think I am a mistake?

What was she even thinking? Her mother had a new family and didn't need her. Her father was the good one, after all.

Iyawa closed her eyes, feeling utterly miserable. "Good. I'd like to go home, please. David must not meet me here. It was nice to see you, Mother."

Chapter Thirteen

The stillness in the cab was so fierce, she could hear Matthias's ragged breathing next to her.

She wanted to speak to him in the vehicle, but she could not. Not that she didn't try, but anytime her mouth opened, a tear would drop. Everything had happened so fast.

As much as her soul sought comfort, she wasn't going to show Matthias how broken she was inside.

He had tried asking her if she was okay, but she couldn't describe what she was feeling.

When the car—a taxi they'd picked up near her mother's place—stopped in front of the hotel, she couldn't be happier to see the magnificent building once again.

Her mind echoed with both her father and mother's voice. Was she really a mistake? Wasn't there any good thing about her that could make someone stay?

No wonder Matthias's mother freaked out when she discovered Iyawa was his fiancée. It was so obvious.

Matthias requested for his card at the check-in suite and was granted.

After he opened the door to the room, Iyawa fell down on the bed. Ah, she couldn't even cry as there were no more tears left.

A familiar feeling of emptiness had crept in, and she wished for it to go.

Snatching the pillow, she screamed into it. Her sorrow was a huge, painful knot inside.

"Iyawa," Matthias called after her. "Would you please tell me what happened?"

She tore herself from the pillow and looked at him. Concern plastered his handsome face, and in that moment of despair, she couldn't help but admire his features. Did he see her as a mistake, too?

"Tell me what is wrong. Just look at how you've been ever since we came back from your mother's place. Did she say anything wrong?"

Iyawa sat in bed and rubbed her forehead. She could feel an eager affection coming from him just as he stared at her, and something intense flared through her.

She gazed down at her fingers. "Matthias?"

"Yes, Iyawa. What is it?" His voice was calm.

She paused and continued in a sinking tone. "Do you ever see me as a damaged person?"

Her words seem to surprise him as he took three steps forward, his eyes jutting out. "What in the world are you talking about?"

"My mother thinks I'm a mistake. I can't help but notice it's the same thing my dad said." There was soreness in her throat.

"You are not a mistake. God doesn't create mistakes. You are a human, and that's not a mistake."

Hot blood ran through her veins. He was trying to sweet-talk her. Why couldn't he just say the truth like everyone else?

She barrelled towards him with flared nostrils. "Don't you try to calm me down. I don't like people lying to me. I'm a mistake. Even the whole world thinks so. Even in church, people still give me the bad eye."

Matthias's eyes narrowed with immense concern.

She pressed a palm over her lips to hold back a cry. "Or is this because of my past? I'm no longer that Iyawa."

"No. That's not it. I told you never to put words in my mouth."

"Then why?! Give me a good reason why everyone hates me!" she screamed, throwing the words at him like stones.

Her annoyance increased when she found out her hands were now shaking. She had never felt this much emotions over a long time.

Iyawa shoved him backward, her heart thumping madly. "Tell me why! Why do all of you treat me like I am some damaged product that can't be repaired? Why?"

"Stop, Iyawa. You are losing control of yourself."

She seethed with mounting rage and humiliation and shoved him backwards again. "You don't tell me what to do."

His mouth dipped into an even deeper frown.

This time, Matthias inched forward and pulled her by the waist, her head against his chest.

She screamed, trying to wiggle out of his hold, but he was stronger. "Let me be, Matthias. I just want to kill myself. I want my mother. I want my mother."

"Iyawa, stop it. Please."

She was soon breathless with rage. Mixed feelings surged through her.

After struggling for a while, she swallowed with difficulty and calmed down, taking slow breaths as she sank into his cushioning embrace.

What have I done? How could I be so vulnerable around him?

"Iyawa, I hear you." Matthias stood still for a while.

She used his chest to hide her face as she trembled with shame and wept aloud. "Why doesn't she want me? Why Matthias? Why?"

She could feel him stroking her hair.

"Your mother? She didn't want you? That's her problem."

The question was a stab in her heart, but she managed to find her voice. "All along, I thought my father was the evil doer, but he saved my life. A...and it hurts. Hurts to know I grew up with memories that weren't true."

"Im, let yourself feel anything you want to feel. It hurts, but I promise you, it is not forever. I am here for you."

"She called me a mistake."

Matthias placed a kiss on her forehead. "Iyawa, I am so sorry. I don't know why your mother said or did what she did, but I know one thing. You are not a mistake. Never. I see you, and I see God's perfection."

"You are saying this just because you feel pity towards me."

"No, Iyawa. I said this because I know you are not a mistake. Act like the devil or monster, I know deep down, there is a broken angel just wanting to be heard. You deserve so much more from people who fail to understand you." He shook his head.

Iyawa could feel warmth spread around her at just the thought of him not viewing her as a mistake. She sniffed back her tears, her heart racing at their closeness. "It seems like this pain won't go away forever. I don't even know what to do."

Matthias pulled back from the hug and wiped her tears with his finger, cupping her face with his big hands. "Whatever you decide to do, I will support you. You wanna shout your mom's name in anger, no problem. You want to get out of here, I understand."

"I am sorry for how I acted earlier. I...I just lost control." She flung herself against him.

He offered a long sigh.

"It is okay. It's fine."

After a long moment of silence, he spoke. "Is this why you were ashamed of your past? Do you think it's because of your mother?"

She trembled with tears. "I don't know what it is seriously. But I remember growing up being a rebellious child. It took my mind off my mother. Now, I think I just messed myself up for nothing. I grew up thinking it is the only thing that can help me through my worries. C...Can I ever back out of this miserable feeling?"

He gave a nod, his eyes boring into hers. "Yes. With time, Iyawa. With time and support from the people you love."

She lowered her gaze. There was so much in his eyes that made her heart flutter.

What is going on in your heart, Iyawa? Why is it that anytime he looks at you, you look away in fear of the unknown?

Matthias Bade was an attractive man with a heart of gold. He cared deeply for her, and this alone made her want to rethink lots of things. The feelings were sharp as she finally admitted the truth.

She didn't hate Matthias anymore. She might have loathed him for helping her father, but right now, what she was feeling wasn't hate.

.. ∞ ..

SHE COULDN'T BE HAVING feelings for Matthias—Iyawa questioned this when she woke up the next morning. It was just five o'clock, yet it seemed like so much time had passed since yesterday. The pains in her heart had lessened, and all she could think of last night was how she felt yesterday.

Iyawa was surprised to find herself placed gently upon his chest as he cuddled her in his sleep. She raised her head with caution to look at his face.

He is even hotter in his sleep.

She shook her head. Matthias would never like someone like her. Her mind flashed to the times he'd shown great care and affection for her. Certainly, he was just one with a good heart. She wasn't supposed to be reading meaning into it.

Ah, yes, she was aware he was kinder than he wanted anyone to know.

She sat up next to him on the bed. She couldn't tear herself from his profile. Could someone like him really like her?

Iyawa slowly curled her fingers in his hair, and he stirred in his sleep.

When he managed to open his eyes, he gave her a smile.

"God, how long have I been sleeping?"

"It is still early."

"Im, are you better now? Why are you awake?"

That was it! She was tired of fighting her own personal restraint.

Without giving another thought, she pressed her lips against his, kissing him tenderly.

Her pulse raced when he returned the kiss.

He pulled away. "Iyawa?"

His look was so galvanizing, it sent tremors through her. For a moment, she thought she detected a flicker in his intimate eyes.

"I am sorry," she said, her cheeks colouring under the hold of his gaze.

He muttered something as he leaned down and kissed her slowly, more urgently.

He took her palm and pressed a kiss in it before saying," I have never kissed anyone like this before."

"Never?"

"Never." A genuine smile came across his face, and his lips slowly descended to meet hers. Matthias could go on kissing her until their lips were swollen, and she wouldn't mind.

"This is the first time I have been kissed like this, too," she said.

His hands found hers, and this time, he smiled.

Chapter Fourteen

When Iyawa woke up in the morning, Matthias wasn't in the room. Last night, they'd talked more about themselves, and she had been the first to sleep.

She rubbed the sleep away from her eyes and inspected the room. He was nowhere to be found.

She was about to drown her head with insecure questions when her sight caught a tray with covered plates and beside them a new cellphone and a neatly folded piece of paper on the bedside table.

She shifted and picked up the tray.

I'm greatly sorry if you don't meet me in the room. I didn't want to wake you up from your slumber.

She found herself blushing as she read on.

Here is a new cellphone I got for you. I am presently with Rari. Need to explain what happened to his car. Enjoy your breakfast in bed!

Her heart fluttered with satisfaction, and even if she knew Matthias couldn't feel things for her the way she was starting to feel, she was grateful for the little moments with him.

After taking her breakfast which was three slices of bread and tea, she began going through the new phone. It was way smaller than her former TeleInc one, but it was a gift from Matthias.

Immediately, she typed in her sister's number, and on the third ring, Jadesola picked up.

"Hello? Who is this?" her sister's soft voice said.

Iyawa cleared her throat. "It is me, Iyawa."

Her sister gave a small gasp.

"Iyawa Jaseth? Is that you? Where are you? Have you been kidnapped? Are they asking for money? How much are they asking? I don't mind coming to SA."

"Whoa. Whoa. Take it easy on me. No one kidnapped me."

"Popsi and I have been worried. For a moment, I was expecting Matthias to come back to Nigeria and say you decided to stay. I was scared."

"I said I wouldn't leave you, remember?" She was now smiling even if Jadesola could not see her.

"I know. We tried calling your number, and it was always disconnected. Same for Matthias. And the fact you are using a different number to call me means something. What happened?"

Iyawa could hear the concern in her tone.

A soft and loving smile touched her lips. "I am okay, stop worrying. Though days ago, I was robbed and left with nothing. I slept in a forest. A forest with creeping insects."

"What? You got robbed and slept in a forest? I hope you were not hurt? Popsi must not get to hear this." Jadesola gasped.

At the mention of her Popsi, her heart sank.

"Relax. I am fine. I just have many things to tell you when I come home." She swallowed. "How is Popsi?"

For a moment, there was silence on the other end.

"Jadesola?"

"Huh? Sorry, I just had to check if I am not in another universe because what the heck?"

"Jadesola, how is Popsi?"

"Popsi is fine. Working so hard for the launching ceremony. It is coming up soon, remember?"

"I remember. How is the company?"

"Going great."

Yes, her sister was difficult with her at times, but it could be they simply just disagreed on the very nature and ways of showing love.

She could hear the sound of Jadesola clearing her throat.

"And your mom? How is she?"

"Doing so fine without me."

"Oh, Im—"

"I don't want to talk about it now. When we meet."

"And the honeymoon?"

Iyawa's heart swelled with a feeling she had thought she couldn't feel. "It is not a honeymoon. We should be back anytime soon."

"We? Iyawa, you rarely use we."

She could hear the confusion in Jadesola's voice.

"Yes, I do. I use it all the time."

"Spill it out. I love juicy things like this."

Iyawa was tongue-tangled for a while. What was she going to say? That they had reached a point where their relationship became an open book?

Jadesola took her hesitation as an indication. "My God! Something did happen? I don't want to make guesses so you better tell me."

Iyawa bit her lower lips as images from this morning flashed through her mind. "When did you realize you loved Benjy?"

"Hmm. Is this about him?"

Iyawa gave a coy smile. "No. I didn't say that. Just answer the question."

She could practically feel Jadesola's smile through the phone.

"I think it was when I couldn't sleep at night. Those days, I created this image of both of us and then I saw the card he gave me for my birthday. I knew I was gone for good. And you, my sister, really like the person on your mind when I was speaking."

Iyawa chewed on her finger. Hearing those words out loud makes her want to check her feelings with fearful clarity.

Could she say she was in love with Matthias or she liked him? She was feeling things she didn't know or couldn't describe, but didn't mean it could be love.

"You know that is not possible. We just had a heart-to-heart talk and became overwhelmed with our emotions," she said. "We kissed."

"You kissed? How did that make you feel? This sounds different, Iyawa."

She rubbed her face. "Jadesola, it feels so right. It was the most wonderful thing that has ever happened to me. It was different from every time I have been with another man."

"Then what's the problem? You said it yourself, it feels right."

Something shattered in her. A realization she might never give herself to any man and not to Matthias who deserved better.

"I am not like other ladies he has been with. You know my past, don't you? Why would he want someone like me? He deserves someone like you."

"You can't decide for him. Iyawa, do you regret your past actions? Are you sober about your past?"

She nodded. "Yes. I did so many things without thinking about my future or anything. But it's too late now."

"What are you saying? It is never late. Talk to him."

When she didn't reply, Jadesola spoke up.

"Oh, dear, you don't know what to do. You've opened your heart."

. . ⚜ . .

TIME PASSED QUICKLY, and Iyawa was dressed in a maroon wool dress with her hair down. It'd been long time since Matthias had left the room, and he wasn't even back yet.

This wasn't okay, because all she could think about was if he had started to regret the kissed they'd shared.

Four hours since she'd woken up. Where was he? Her lips thinned in displeasure as she paced the room.

It was really stupid for her to feel like this. What was wrong with her?

Iyawa started to head for the door, finally making a decision to take a long walk. When she opened the door, she was startled to find Matthias standing on the other side.

He stopped abruptly, first looking at the ground, then letting his gaze drift up to her face. He was dressed in jeans and a jacket, staring at her with those beautiful dark eyes that sent a delicious shiver along her backbone.

"Iyawa, I can see you are awake," he said, a blush creeping onto his cheeks.

She smiled, closing the door before her. "Yes, I am. Why didn't you wake me up, and where have you been?"

"I thought you might want to sleep. Last night was too much for you."

She massaged her arm in circles. "I wasn't that tired. Crying can't drain your strength. You left me all bored here with a letter."

"I wrote that letter with my best handwriting." He chuckled. "I had to explain things to Rari about his car."

"Did he take it well? His car?"

He shrugged. "He did a pretty good job at understanding me. I just have to send money for compensation. Also, he invited me for his wife's birthday party this evening. She is dying to meet you."

"No qualms. I mean, I have nothing doing anyways."

He followed her as she ambled down the hallway. "Where are you going?"

"I don't really know. Maybe going on a long walk."

"Great. We can both go for a long walk," he said. "Except if you want to be alone in the meantime. I understand."

She felt the heat of a blush on her cheeks. "No. I'd love for you to come."

When they got out of the hotel and into the streets to explore the beauty of the surroundings, a soft breeze picked up her hair, stirring the strands around her cheeks.

The street was redolent with tall and magnificent buildings, cars lined up beside the walkway. Boutiques, shopping malls, companies stood in glory, all complimenting the beauty of the town. People were walking on the walkway getting on with their business.

The stillness between them lasted for a minute, and she could guess each was trying to gather his or her thoughts.

"I have many questions. Are we talking about the kiss? Are we staying here or going home?"

She chuckled. "I liked the kiss. Did you?"

"The kiss was good. I loved it." He blushed.

"We like each other, so what does it mean?"

Matthias looked at her. "Isn't it obvious? We have this connection together."

"Just a connection?"

Connection was a simpler word that held no complications, so she could manage with it.

He let out a breath. "I also don't know what this is. We like being around each other. I don't know what that means. I don't want us to jump to conclusions only to hurt one another."

"What do you think this is? Should we just leave it as it is or explore this connection we have?"

He smiled at her. "It might just be something temporary between us. I am sure after this engagement is over, you will puke when you think of us kissing. Let's just enjoy the moment. Do you want to explore?"

A part of her didn't agree with his comment, but why risk this moment? "If you are ready, then why not?"

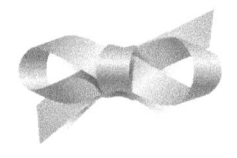

Chapter Fifteen

"Hang on. Let me get this straight." She sucked through the straw. "You have seen both your grandparents? Maternal and paternal?"

Matthias nodded. "And my great-grandmother. I bet you've never seen yours?"

Iyawa chuckled. Being here with Matthias on a date in this big smoothie shop in SA wasn't something she'd expected would happen earlier. "Never have I heard or seen them. They are all dead."

"Ouch."

She rolled her eyes. "Another question."

He placed his cup on the table and crossed his arms. "Favourite memory of your Popsi?"

She tried to search through her memories, slowly sucking the smoothie out of the straw.

"Hmm, there aren't much, you can tell. I think my favourite memory with my Popsi would be when we decided to light up fireworks during a particular New Year's Eve. I don't know who came up with the idea, and Jadesola wasn't born then. She was still in the belly and....and that day, I almost burnt myself while playing with the fire, and he was angry. He put the fire out, hugged me, and just stayed there patting my hair. Ever since then, he banned me from playing with fireworks."

Iyawa could still remember how angry both her father and Aunt Madeline had been then.

Matthias gave her a serious look. "Seriously, what happened to you two?"

"I also don't know. Maybe I frustrated the man while growing up, and he frustrated me, too. We have a love-hate relationship."

"Hmm. That isn't healthy. Things needs to change between you two."

"Enough about my boring relationship with my dad. What about you? What memories of your father do you cherish?"

"Ah, there are much. We are pretty close. My favourite memory of Dad would be the random nights he used to surprise us, me and my sister, with his special, delicious midnight snacks. We would just be sleeping and wake up to a bowl of donuts, egg rolls, scotch eggs. I really miss all that."

"Your father can cook?"

He nodded. "He is a great chef."

"My father wouldn't even know how to switch on gas if he was in front of a stove. All his life, he has had his personal chefs and all." Iyawa laughed.

"Not every man can cook. I can't cook. You also can't, remember? And you are a woman."

She raised her high chin. "I have been taking lessons."

"From who?"

She could draw out the surprise in his voice.

"Someone. My turn now. What is the most embarrassing thing you can remember that has happened to you?"

"No way I am answering that. I've done so many embarrassing things."

She shoved him in a playful manner. "Of course you have. You are Matthias, after all. Hey, you have to tell me one of them. It can't be all that bad."

"Fine. There was this day I was going to my father's office, and I took the elevator. The coffee I had didn't go well with my stomach so I silently farted in the elevator."

Iyawa's eyes flew wide as she burst into a peal of laughter. "Disgusting! How could you?"

"I didn't know there was going to be a reaction, but it was so bad, everyone else around started reacting to it. No one could even look at me because I was the son of the CEO. They even apologized for putting me in a discomforting position." Matthias relaxed, joining in the smile.

"You are so bad! You are worse than me! Your story is worse than mine."

"Shut up! Tell me you haven't gone through something embarrassing like that."

She shook her head. "No, I don't fart in public. The one embarrassing thing would be when I was invited to a charity event with Jadesola, and I wore this sleeveless long dress, but unfortunately, I couldn't make it inside."

"Don't tell me you died." Matthias placed his hand on his chest.

"Shut up. I was going on, smiling and waving as the media took my pictures, when someone stepped on my hem, and my dress was almost pulled down. It turned out the zip was worn out. Jadesola and my father's bodyguards covered me up back into the car. I wanted to cry."

"Jeez! That is so bad. What did you do when you got home?"

"I burnt it. I didn't buy from that designer again."

Matthias laughed.

"Are you more of an outdoor person or indoor? You seem indoorish."

"Indoorish is not a word. You know me, I love adventures. I am an outdoor person."

"Countries you've been to?"

"Germany, USA, UK, India, Ghana, South Africa. I think that's all. What about you?"

"I am in between the lines of outdoor personality and indoor. I've been to Spain, Mexico, China, and Costa Rica. But they are all mainly for business."

Matthias laughed. "Okay, next question."

"Your favourite food?"

"Jollof rice with chicken."

"Not bad. Give me yam porridge with efo, the vegetable soup, and you have won my heart." She licked her lips.

"Yam porridge and efo. I'll remember that."

Iyawa's cheeks coloured a shade of red. "Hobbies?"

"Reading mystery books and sometimes non-fiction. You?"

"Drawing, and yes, reading books."

Matthias leaned back on the chair, his eyes sparkling as they watched her. "I have a new hobby, though."

Her heartbeat was still steady. *For now.*

"I like being with you, Iyawa."

She was in cloud nine before she realized she had to say it back, and she didn't hold back.

· · ⚜ · ·

THE NIGHT OF THE PARTY came sooner than she expected. When Iyawa glanced down through the window blinds, she could see various cars parked in front of the hotel.

Wow, this is very big for a birthday party.

"Iyawa, are you dressed?"

She turned at the call of her name.

Matthias looked handsome but nervous as he approached her. He wore a button-down shirt and black pants.

"Yes, you called?"

His eyes gleamed with delight. "You look pretty in that gown!"

She glanced down at her dress. She wore a plum purple body con dress that made her look beautiful.

Iyawa's heart pounded frantically as Matthias observed her for the last time.

"Thank you. You don't look bad yourself," she replied.

When they got to the hall, she could hear murmuring and smell scents of different perfumes as they found their way among the crowd. It was so big, with people dressed in elegant outfits as they walked around.

The ceiling was very high with a huge crystal chandelier hanging from it. Cream pillars stood with vases of blossoms giving off a scent to set the atmosphere.

"Look, Rari is there with his wife." Matthias pointed to a corner where Rari stood in front of a huge white fountain cake with a fair-skinned lady.

When they approached the duo, Rari and Matthias shared a hug. She exchanged a smile with the fair-skinned lady who she guessed to be his wife.

"How are you, Iyawa?" Rari asked. "You are looking radiant, as always."

"I am good. This is such a lovely party! Way to go," she commented.

"I take no praise!" Rari held his wife's hand. "This is all my wife's idea. She plans her parties. Zola, this is Iyawa. Matthias's fiancée. Iyawa, my wife, Zola."

Zola took Iyawa's hand. "Nice to meet you, Iyawa. I must comment, you are very beautiful. Matthias really has eyes for choosing you."

"Thank you. I couldn't stop staring at your dress. It was made just for you."

And she wasn't lying. The white, feathery gown Zola wore complimented her features so well.

"I am the birthday girl, after all. No one should steal my thunder."

Rari patted his wife's back. "Honey, why don't you get to know Iyawa more? I am just going to introduce Matthias to someone."

Her throat seized up at the mention of someone.

Matthias nodded. "I will be right back. Have fun, Iyawa."

Both ladies watched as the men retreated from their sight. She couldn't help but wonder what they were going to do.

"How are you? How is SA treating you?" Zola turned to her, eyes sparkling with warmth.

"Good. I love SA. Did you grow up here?"

"Yes. I heard you guys came for a mini-vacation. That is so sweet. How did you two meet each other?"

Ah, Zola was one of those people who loved to hear the stories of how couples met. Her mind retraced to the first day they saw each other.

"We met at a party. Our fathers are friends. I thought he was attractive and walked up to him telling him so."

Zola placed a hand over her mouth. "You are so brave. I don't think I have it in me to do something like that. Rari said Matthias finds you daring and brave. That is really sweet if you ask me. I want to be this way someday."

The fact Matthias had thought of her as daring and brave squeezed her heart a little bit. What happened to him thinking she was sweet, lovable, and all?

"Not really sweet per se. He rejected me." Iyawa shrugged. "And I slapped him."

"What?"

She chuckled at Zola's expression. It was exciting forming up a story of how she had met Matthias. "Don't worry, we met four years later. He was the one who did the pursuing, trust me. One thing led to another, and we fell in love. Months later, he put the ring on it."

"That is so cute. I am happy for you two." Zola gave her a tiny squeeze of the hand. "Marriage can be daunting at times. I won't lie to you. You will want to kill each other. You will want to do things that will hurt one another. Everyday won't be Valentine's Day, trust me, but when you look at the whole reason you married him, you will realize love covers it all."

Iyawa's heart grew a little warmth as she nodded. "Thank you. How did you meet Rari?"

"He was my ex-boyfriend's best friend." Zola's face coloured. "I was still with my ex then."

"Oh my gosh. Talk about daring and brave. How did you even get with him?"

"My ex missed our six-month-anniversary for a football game, and he told Rari to come apologize to me because he couldn't face me." Zola snorted. "What a coward! Well, I thought Rari was cute as he sat on my couch then, telling me reasons why I should forgive my ex. Things happened, we fell in love, and I broke up with my ex who sent me a message calling me names. Come on, he missed our six-month-anniversary for a stupid game."

Iyawa cocked her head in surprise. "You are on a real level of boldness. I am your student now, teacher."

"Oh, you flatter me. It is just...it is just that we can't stop love when it happens. It is always unexpected and happens with the one person we would never think of."

Her mind flashed with Matthias's name. Iyawa tried shaking her thoughts off. There was never anything that could result in him loving her. He liked kissing her, is all.

Zola chuckled, turning her gaze to the huge cake. "So tell me, Iyawa dear, what do you think of this cake?"

"I think it's lovely." Iyawa looked at the layers of white cake with flower designs and fondants. "And very, very big."

"Big, yes. Just lovely? What about the designs and lettering? I think it's so over the top."

Iyawa thought so, too, and was about to comment when something caught her eye. A beautiful woman in a gold mermaid dress sashayed in, gaining everyone's attention, including Matthias. The woman had this aura of confidence like the big gold chain resting on her neck. Behind her were men dressed in black suits with shades on.

From a corner, she could see Rari leading Matthias up to the woman. By now, every head had returned to their business, just few still staring at the lady.

Her stomach tied into a knot when the woman's hand lingered too long on Matthias's back, and she laughed as a result of something he said to her.

He really seems to be enjoying himself.

"Who is this lady?" she asked Zola.

Zola plucked a glass of champagne from a passing waiter. "That is Demi."

Iyawa resisted the urge to frown. Too bland and answer for her liking.

"Um, sorry, but why is everyone looking at her like she is some goddess?'

"Because she is a goddess. Demi is a big philanthropist here in SA. She is Rari's friend." Zola's smile widened.

Iyawa caught herself glancing over her shoulder. What was she doing?

"Do you want to meet her? She is very nice."

"No. There is no need. I will meet her sometime."

Zola greeted some guest passing by. "Iyawa, I hope you don't mind. I have to go greet some of my friends who came for my party. Are you okay with being by yourself?"

"Yes. You go on, birthday girl."

Minutes after Zola had gone, Iyawa was leaning on the pillar, sipping her drink, when someone breathed on her neck from behind. Slow music was on, and some people were now dancing with their partners while some were still talking and chatting. From a corner, she could see Zola chatting with some ladies and Rari attending to a guest, but no sign of Matthias or the goddess.

Her grip on the glass tightened, her long white fingernails ready to dig in.

"I wish I was that glass," Matthias said to her, placing a peck on her left cheek.

She turned to look at him, her lips thinned. "Be careful what you wish for. I am halfway to breaking this glass."

She wanted to ignore him for letting her stay here all by herself while he chatted with a new friend of his, but looking at his face again, a part of her blushed at the peck.

"Calm down, Miss Feisty. The music is on. You care to have a dance with me?" he asked, bowing in a dramatic way.

Iyawa hesitated, sizing him up. "Why? You didn't find anyone else to dance with you?"

He leaned in again to give a brief kiss on the lips. "I can find anyone here to dance with me, but I have no connection with them. I want you instead."

She didn't want to fight this desire to be close to him again. "Then dance with me, you stupid."

She dropped the glass on the table, and Matthias's hand gripped her waist, drawing her closer to eternal life. She looked up at him, and excitement leaped from within her.

"You look so beautiful in purple. I couldn't take my eyes away from you," he whispered in her ear, using his tongue to tease the tip of her ear as they moved slowly.

She could feel the heat emanating from him. It was like it was just the two of them in the room. "Who said I wasn't also staring?"

A tap on her shoulder caused her to pull away. "Sorry to disturb. Can I have this dance with your fiancé?"

Iyawa regarded Matthias with curiosity. Demi had walked up to them, asking to dance with him.

His eyes widened, his hands finally leaving her waist. "Oh, I—"

"I don't think she will mind. Can I have this dance, please?" Demi pouted.

She waited for Matthias to speak up and say he cannot leave her, but he said nothing, staring at her like he was waiting for her reply. She knew their engagement was fake, but she so wanted to shove her ring in Demi's face.

She forced a smile. "Of course. Why not?"

"Are you sure?" Matthias raised an inquisitive eyebrow.

"Yes. I was just about to get another drink."

Iyawa stood there, watching Matthias move so closely with another woman. She watched and watched until she couldn't bear it. Without sparing another glance, she left the hall.

Chapter Sixteen

Underneath her bed cover, Iyawa tried not to think about the events of the party. She wasn't like Demi. The sweet, charming young lady who just happened to charm everyone. Iyawa knew she was far different, and that was what scared her.

When she removed the bed cover from her head, she flinched at the tall, dark figure at the door.

"You almost scared me," she said, using her hand to remove strands of her hair from her face. "You have twenty seconds to explain what you are doing here standing so creepily."

His voice was gentle. "You left the party."

"Why do you care?"

"I was looking for you and couldn't find you. I was scared. Why did you leave?"

She rolled her eyes. "Again, why do you care? I am okay, as you've seen."

Matthias let out a sigh and approached her. He sat on the edge of the bed. There was this mischievous glint in his eyes as he stared down at her.

"I was getting pretty bored, and I left. Is that a problem?" She tried not to think about the tone she was using.

"I am sorry I left you all alone."

"It is fine. I am sure you enjoyed yourself with that Demi lady. She is a good dancer, isn't she?"

Matthias bit his lower lip. "You told me to dance with her. I asked you if you were okay with it."

"I wasn't expecting you to do it. See the way she interrupted our dance so she could have hers."

"I like it when you are jealous."

She tried ignoring the dazzling current flowing through her.

"I don't get jealous. I get irritated by stupid things. You left me all alone in that party and went on dancing with—"

Matthias leaned down and pressed a kiss on her forehead. "I am sorry for leaving you all alone. Rari wanted me to meet her because she is a close friend of his. We talked about few meaningless things, that's all. I don't even know why she came looking for me on the dance floor. I thought you were okay with it."

"I didn't say I wasn't."

He chuckled and moved to kiss the tip of her nose. "I know. Why don't we take the next flight to Nigeria tomorrow? What do you think?"

Iyawa sighed. "I want to visit a beach. After that, we leave. I mean, I have no business here again. My mother is happy with her life. I want to go back home. But after you take me to the beach."

"The beach it is, then." Matthias's eyes sparkled with delight.

· · ~⚘~ · ·

THE NEXT DAY WHEN THEY arrived at Sandwha Beach, Iyawa couldn't believe her eyes. It was like the biggest beach she had ever seen. As she laid there on the blue deck chair Zola had lent her, under a big umbrella shading a few other chairs, she couldn't help but forget all her worries for a while.

She could listen to the quiet whoosh of the waves moving through the water, the wind in her ears, people clapping and laughing, birds squawking, even the squealing and splashing from the kids running around.

She had her reading glasses on, and a mystery novel she had stopped reading was flattened out on her tummy. If there was one thing she loved watching with Jadesola, it was mystery documentaries. There was just something about being killed and not knowing who did it to grasp her attention. The moment leading up to the investigation and discovery served as escapism for her.

She was about to turn back to her mystery book when her eyes caught hold of someone familiar.

Iyawa's mouth dropped. She squinted her gaze at the image in front of her. Wait...was it Matthias?

Yes, it was. She'd recognized the blue shorts he had worn this morning. How did he look so handsome?

Matthias was coming out of the water, droplets sprinkling down his body to his abs. It seemed like the world had stopped for a bit, with imaginary music playing as he walked out of the sea and onto the sand.

She bit her lip, dropping her glasses to cover her eyes. She straightened her shoulders and cleared her throat as he approached her.

He stood over her, his hands on his hips. "I saw you staring."

"Who? Me?"

He rolled his eyes. "You were gaping. Don't be shy."

"Ew....I don't get shy. I wasn't staring. End of discussion." She lifted her glasses up.

"Fine. I will pretend as if I didn't see you." A little smirk appeared on his face. "Get up and come to the water. You will love it."

She shook her head. "I am okay. How long have you been gone? I thought you'd been carried away by the water. Not that I care."

Matthias grabbed the towel on the seat next to her and dropped down beside her. "Ha ha ha. That is so funny. Just come and try the water. Do not tell me you are scared."

"Boo, I don't get scared. I just ain't in the mood for water." She closed her book.

"Iyawa, come on. Wait, what are you reading?" He gasped as he grabbed her book.

"*How to get away with killing*," she replied simultaneously with him.

"You've read this before?"

He nodded. "Yes. I mean, this book is the best. I didn't know you read mystery novels."

"I live for mystery novels. The fact one could murder his wife and try his possible best to escape punishment all through the novel is endearing, sorry if it sounds bizarre."

Matthias scoffed. "Bizarre? Iyawa, I have read so much psychopath novels, I find myself acting out the scenes of an investigator sometimes."

She laughed. "I seriously thought I was the only one. There was this one novel I read. It was about the murder of a teenage girl, and I found myself acting as the investigator at times."

"Let me guess, the name of the novel is *What lies behind Weldon's Street*?"

She shook her head in amusement. "Wow. I am so speechless right now. You love my books."

"What is not to love about them?"

Sweet Matthias! What are you doing to me?

She laughed.

"You are beautiful. I just wanted you to know that."

She blushed. She really was falling hard.

Chapter Seventeen

The flight home was more dramatic than when they arrived. A part of her was in pieces over the fact her reunion with her mother hadn't gone on as she planned. She was leaving her mother. Another part of her was excited about the new development between her and Matthias.

"Bye bye to South Africa." Iyawa looked out the window during take-off.

Matthias brushed his hand across her cheek. "Just so you know, your mother does not deserve you."

"I know. She doesn't. I hope she is happy with her family," she choked out.

"You are sweet, Iyawa. Your mother made a choice even when she wasn't supposed to choose. That's cowardice."

She huffed out a breath. "No, I am not. I am far away from sweet."

"Yes, you are," he said, emphasizing each of the words.

Her shoulders dropped with a sigh. "No, I am not. I could have known she didn't want me. Just because my father never talks about my birth doesn't make him bad."

"Relax. You were torn, Iyawa. It is normal."

His eyes seemed to make her heart beat faster than usual.

"It is not. I don't think I can ever forgive myself." And she wasn't lying.

"You should forgive yourself and your father. And your mother."

Her chest tightened. "Easy for you to say."

"Right. Listen to me. There was a shirt I used to have in my wardrobe that I haven't been able to wear all these years."

"A shirt?"

"Yes, a shirt."

She tilted her head to the side. "What happened with the shirt?"

"Have you seen me with any friends or even talk about any friends? No, right?" Matthias paused to examine her expression. "Because that shirt is the only memory I have of my best friend."

She paused, letting the information sink. It wasn't that she hadn't noticed he rarely talked about friends, but she'd felt it was just his wish.

"Only memory?"

"My friend Jamilah died two years ago. I...I was there the day she died. I saw it with my eyes."

There was so much pain in his voice, she could only watch him with intense curiosity. Was this how she'd sounded when she'd found out about her mother?

"Matthias, I am sorry. How did she die?" Her words came out like a whisper.

His black eyes were filled with pain that glowed. "We were on the phone that fateful night when her cooking gas exploded. It seemed she had been on the phone while cooking in the kitchen. She lived at a dwelling unit in one of these high-rise apartment building with storeys, and people were injured. When I got there, I screamed and cried out for her, but I was held back from going in. When she was wheeled out of the building, she had burns beyond recognition. Not only her, but two other people, including a child."

"That is so sad to hear. She doesn't deserve that." Iyawa's heart sank.

He nodded, his voice cracking as he spoke. "I was hurt, Iyawa. Pained, I grew in misery and anguish. More importantly, I was angry at myself. I blamed myself for their deaths and didn't make contact with humans for months. If she wasn't talking to me that night, she could have made it."

"You didn't do anything, Matthias. You couldn't have changed things even if you wanted. People go, and people come. We can only continue to love them in their absence."

"Perhaps. Everything I could hold on to for memories went with her that night. The shirt was the only thing to remind me of her. She gave it to me on my last birthday. Iyawa, I could not forgive myself."

Her face contorted into confusion. How, then, did he live his life like he didn't have problems?

"How do you try to be happy after what happened? After everything, you still put a smile on."

"Because I went for therapies. I promised myself Jamilah wouldn't want me to live a life filled of misery. She wasn't like that. So every day, I try to forgive myself and live with my pain. Sometimes, yes, I do find myself in situations where I extremely want to render help because I can't afford to hurt anyone, but I am ten times better than then."

"I am sorry for your loss. I bet she is looking down at you, proud of the decisions you took."

"I'm sure you need to forgive yourself, too. You've been through a lot." He gave her an encouraging smile.

"Don't be stupid. I couldn't have done it without you."

Matthias leaned forward, placing his hand on hers. "With or without me, something would have nudged you to see your mother for who she is. You are too smart for that."

Iyawa swallowed tightly as he pulled away. She tried to deny the quiver surging through her body, but it wasn't as easy. Whatever she was feeling for Matthias was intensifying every minute. He made her feel in a way no one had ever made her feel.

A question tugged at her heart. Was he feeling these things, too? Did he feel like the whole world revolved around the two of them when he looked at her? When they were near each other, how did he feel? And the question she didn't want to ask herself: Was she in love with Matthias Bade?

Time passed, and soon, he was leaning his head on the seat, eyes closed. She studied his dark-skinned face. It was then she realized something that caused a fight scene in her brain. She had only a few days left with Matthias. They were supposed to be together for three months, and after the launching of TeleInc latest phone, they'd be able to separate if they wanted. Except she didn't.

What if he doesn't want you to go, too?

"Matthias?" she called.

His eyes were still closed. "Yes?"

Do you think you are in love with me the way I think I am in love with you? she so wanted to say. What was the worst thing that could come out of his mouth? He was a nice person, and even his rejection wouldn't be so harsh.

"Are you falling asleep on me now?" she asked instead.

He chuckled. "Urm...Kind of. I am pretty tired right now. Is that your question?"

"No."

"Go on, then."

"I want to see a therapist. Not because it helped you or anything, but because I think I need to."

All her life, she had made bad choices. Choices that threatened to ruin her reputation and even her father's company. It was time for her to take a new leap.

"Well, that is swell."

· · ⚜ · ·

ONCE THE PLANE HAD landed and Iyawa got her bags, she breathed in the air and couldn't be happier to be in Nigeria again. She missed Jadesola, and even if she hadn't thought she would be saying this, she missed her dad.

Walking out of the airport with Matthias dragging his luggage behind, they met his driver standing beside his car.

"Hey," Matthias greeted the driver. "How have you been?"

The driver collected the luggage from them and placed it into the boot. "Good, sir. How was the vacation?"

"South Africa was the vacation of a lifetime," he replied, giving him a little pat on his shoulder.

"We are just going to go back to our boring lives?" she asked when they got into the car.

Matthias placed a hand on his chest and feigned offence. "We have boring lives? I didn't know."

"You know what I mean."

"I don't know if my life is boring, but I know I want to spend the remaining days having fun with you," he said.

The words he said were enough to make her jump with excitement, but the way he whispered those words to her slapped her with a reality check. He really was planning to leave her after the time had elapsed.

She took a breath and managed a smile. "You are right. We should spend the remaining days together."

"Is anything wrong?"

She shook her head. "No, of course not. It is just that time passed so quickly."

"I know, right. Three months would be coming to an end."

Iyawa nodded. "Feels like it."

"Hey, why don't I take you out for dinner tonight? Should I come pick you up?"

"You want to take me out for dinner? Like just the two of us? Alone?"

Matthias smiled. "Yes. Unless you want to invite your dad, yeah."

"I would love to, stupid."

"Why do you always call me stupid?"

"Because you are stupid. Very very. You even have a stupid face."

"I love it when you call me stupid."

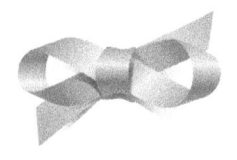

Chapter Eighteen

"Jadesola, that was your favourite mug," Iyawa said when she entered her sister's office.

Jadesola was seated in front of her computer, holding her favourite pink mug which she'd dropped to the ground as soon as she saw Iyawa.

After the outing with Matthias the day before, she'd decided to visit Jadesola in her office but hadn't expect her to break her favourite mug. When she got home yesterday, neither Jadesola nor her dad had been home. Her father was rarely home, but Jadesola?

Jadesola stared at the broken pieces of the mug on the floor and back to her sister.

"You loved this mug. How are you ever going to get a mug you will love so much?"

Jadesola's hand was covering her mouth, her eyes widening in surprise. "I love you—forget about the stupid mug. How are you not in SA? How did you get here?"

"I am not in SA because I am now in Nigeria. I thought it was obvious."

"How did you get here?" Jadesola wasn't going to back out.

Iyawa chuckled as she took a seat in front of her sister. "I took the plane. Why are you asking questions with obvious answers?"

"Shut up. You know that's not what I meant. Of course you took the plane. I...you didn't tell me you were coming."

"Careful with those pieces on the floor. Don't hurt yourself."

"Duhhh. I am wearing boots." Jadesola gave her the who-cares gesture.

That was a first. Jadesola didn't like boots. Iyawa had tried getting her a pair, but she wouldn't take them. And if Jadesola had gotten any new one, she would be the first to know.

Iyawa leaned back in her seat. "Jadesola Jaseth, are you wearing one of my old boots?"

"Yes."

"I thought 'you don't like boots,'" She air-quoted with her fingers.

"I don't. You've been trying to get me to wear one, and this—" Jadesola gave a glimpse at her feet. "It fits perfectly. Back to the question. You didn't tell me you were coming."

"I did. I said I was coming back to Nigeria."

"No, you didn't."

"I am pretty sure I did."

"You weren't specific. At all. You didn't say when."

"I know. I felt I should surprise you."

Jadesola beamed. "Surprise me? I am ecstatic. God knows I love you so much."

Warmth radiated through her chest. Here was someone who loved her despite everything, and they didn't even share the same mother. "Jadesola, have I ever told you how much I love you?"

"You say it all the time. I am just so happy to see you. Oh, I missed you. When did you arrive?"

"Yesterday morning. I didn't meet you at home."

"Yesterday morning?" Jadesola pulled a face of shock. "And you didn't call me or even send a text? I was out with a new friend. We had a sleepover. She is so nice."

Iyawa grew flustered as images of her dinner with Matthias surged into her mind. But she couldn't tell Jadesola. Her sister's hopes would get high, and Iyawa knew it was just for a while.

"I am sorry. Can you just forget it? I was tired. How has work at the office been? Gist me. I want to know what I missed."

Jadesola fiddled with the papers on the table. "Nothing much. Preparations are in gear for the launching. Popsi has been shouting and yelling about the arrangements and all. Everything we do isn't right for him."

"Really?" Iyawa wrinkled her nose. If her father had been in a bad mood two weeks away from the launching, something must have put him in such a mood.

"Err...Yes. He once argued with the staff that the hall planning for the event wasn't good, and I saw no wrong in it."

Her stomach tightened. This was her job. She was supposed to work with their event planners to make the day a perfect one, but she had been so caught up in her own drama. That day, reputable people were going to be there, and her father wouldn't want to flunk it.

"I know why he is angry. That's what I was supposed to take care of, if I was here."

"I don't think it's why he is angry. I mean, Derin and Co has been planning events for us for a long time now. You remember the seminar on AIDs sponsored by us? The hall was cool, and we didn't even assist in anything. They know the taste of TeleInc already. That's no problem."

"Why is he angry, then?"

Jadesola swivelled in her seat, pointing a finger at her sister. "I think our Popsi missed you. Like he didn't like the way you weren't here."

Iyawa let out a silly snort. "Yeah. I am also pregnant."

"You slept with Matthias?" Jadesola's eyes widened in disbelief. "And you are now pregnant?"

Iyawa gave an incredulous stare, hiding her blush in the process. "Dude, that was a joke. I...I didn't sleep with Matthias."

"Iyawa." Jadesola's brow knitted into a frown. "It is not funny."

"What? I thought we were joking saying Popsi can even miss me. That's ridiculous."

Jadesola's eyes screamed disapproval. "Popsi missed you."

"Jadesola, I know—"

"I am not making it up. Can you believe just last week, he told me to ask Iyawa to send the drafted proposal to forward to that camera company? I was surprised, and I had to explain Iyawa was on a vacation." Jadesola's mouth twisted into a smile.

Iyawa shrugged to hide her disbelief. There was no way her father would think of her while she was gone. But Jadesola had not reason to lie to her. "You are kidding. I know you are. Look at your eyes, they are twitching. You can't keep a straight face if you are lying."

Jadesola batted her eyelashes. "Those twitching eyes mean I am tired. Not everyone was on a vacation."

"I still don't believe you."

"I am not telling a lie. I swear on my mother's grave. I am not joking."

Jadesola would never joke with her mother's name. Growing up, her sister wished she knew much about her mother before she died. It wouldn't make much sense to be joking with such.

"You are not telling a lie."

"I am not."

"I don't even know what to say."

"It is fine. You should see him. I bet he is yelling at one of the staff."

Iyawa didn't say anything.

"How far with your mom? You still haven't told me anything yet."

Iyawa's stomach flopped. "That...didn't go well."

"What happened? I don't understand."

Iyawa took a deep breath and tried to relax as she poured out the story of what went down.

When she was done, Jadesola just sat there, blank and with an open mouth. "Did this really happen? Are you kidding me?"

"I wish I was." Her voice was lower than she could have imagined.

She watched Jadesola's eyes widen in concern as her sister sprung to her feet. Jadesola enveloped her in a bear hug as soon as she got to where she was seated.

"Your mother did this to you? How could she? You love her. She is a bad person."

Iyawa stared blindly away, tears trembling on her eyelids. "That is so true. She is not a good person. My mother is not a good person. I mean, I don't even know if she is good."

"I am so sorry. I...I don't even know what to say."

"I also don't know what to say. All my life, I wanted to see her, but it is like she didn't want me."

Jadesola cupped her cheeks. "I want you. I love you, and I cannot imagine life without you. You are my big sis, Iyawa."

Iyawa smiled but didn't answer. How could she leave someone who loved her dearly this way? It wasn't just possible.

"And I can't believe you have another sister and even a brother in SA. I am jealous, you know." Jadesola scoffed.

"I don't have another sister. You are my only sister. Those are my mother's kids."

Jadesola straightened, her eyes sizing up Iyawa. "And Matthias?"

"What about Matthias?"

"Nothing. Just wanted you to know the whole engagement sham ends after the launching of TeleInc Spark 10." Jadesola's eyes sat her still on the chair. "Except you don't want it to end."

Her heart stuttered as the confirmation set in. This engagement between her and Matthias was really going to stop. "I don't get what you mean. It was a scheme to get people off my back. People bought it. It has to end."

"You know I can read you, right? Your mouth is saying you don't care, but your heart is saying something different." Jadesola's voice came out gentle.

Iyawa didn't want to ask, but she found herself asking. "What do you think my heart is saying?"

"I don't know. What do *you* think your heart is saying?"

The realization poked and tickled her. Right there on the chair, her mind retraced to the moments she'd had with Matthias. He made her feel in a way no one ever did. She wanted to be with him, and just the thought of not seeing him after the launching ceremony made her tummy turn. He was there for her when she needed him the most, and he didn't take advantage of her when she was in her most vulnerable state. No one made her feel this way.

"I...I have feelings for him." She looked up at her sister as realization washed over her. "Feelings...feelings like love."

There it was. She couldn't deny the truth anymore. The harder she tried ignoring it, the longer it stayed. Iyawa thought this would calm her down, but a variety of thoughts began rumbling in her head.

Jadesola sighed in relief. "I thought you were going to deny it. I am so happy. You love someone."

"Jadesola, this is not good. I...I love Matthias. That is not good." Her muscles were now tense.

"I don't think I grab. Why is this not good?"

"What if he doesn't love me back? I don't even know if he feels the same way."

"Come on. He follows you to find your mother? Sounds like a guy in love."

She shook her head. "Sounds like typical Matthias. Matthias is always like that with everyone. He is this kind, sweet guy. He is that person, Jadesola."

"I say, it is different. You can't just decide. Tell him."

"I have slept with so many men, Jadesola. Why would he want someone like me? I don't fit him, and you know it."

Jadesola's eyebrows slanted in a frown. "I only know you are doing all the decision-making."

"I have to go assist Popsi with the planning." Iyawa rose to her feet. "See you at lunch."

"You don't want to hear me out. Just tell him."
"No."

· · ⚜ · ·

IYAWA CRACKED HER KNUCKLES, staring at the door to her father's office. She looked at his name, gripping the blue file containing all the final arrangements.

She swallowed and knocked. There was no response the first time. She knocked again. The thought of her father missing her clouded her mind.

"Come in," he said.

"Hello, Popsi."

Her father's eyes lit up when he saw her. He had his reading glasses on as he sat in front of his TeleInc laptop. "I...Iyawa."

"Good to see you, too, Popsi. When last did I see you?" She snorted.

His eyebrows pulled up a frown. "When did you leave South Africa? You could have called. I wasn't home yesterday."

"Hey. No greetings. No welcome hugs. That's no way to greet your daughter who you haven't seen for days."

For a moment, she thought she saw something like light flicker through his dark eyes. Her father let out a breath, relaxed in his seat, and took off his glasses.

"Welcome back, Iyawa. When did you get back from South Africa? You could have come to the office, you know. Your sister has been the one helping a lot."

And he is back. She bit down on her teeth. How could she be stupid? Her father didn't miss her. He was just angry she had not been doing any work.

Iyawa stomped to the table and plopped the blue file down on his table. "The designs for the events have been finalized. I have done all the necessary things. If you have anything else for me, let me know."

"You've finalized everything? That's great. I can feel this event is going to be a big one—"

Her nostrils flared as she stared down at him. "Yeah. I have to go now. You can dwell in the wine of your success when I am gone."

"Wait. Why are you angry?"

"Me? Who says I am angry? Do I look angry?" Her temper was higher than ever.

"Watch your tone, young lady. What is wrong? I was just about to congratulate you for a job well done."

She resisted the urge to roll her eyes. Every time, it was a job well done. She could speak now or keep her mouth shut for ever.

"You are not the best father, you know?"

"Ehn?"

"A little part of me was excited when Jadesola said you missed me while I was gone. God, I didn't want to believe it, but I did. I didn't even know what I was expecting when I came here. I...I don't even know what to say anymore. I love Jadesola, but I guess I am not her." Her voice cracked. She shouldn't have brought in her sister's name.

Her father tilted his head to the side and pursed his lips. "I don't understand what you mean by you are not her? It is sounding somehow in my head."

"Forget it. A slip of tongue." She took two steps back.

"Which is strange, because you are always sure of what to say. You are my daughter. Don't think I didn't notice."

"I am your daughter?" She scoffed. "I am the daughter you don't love. It is so obvious you love Jadesola better."

Her father gave a dismissive chuckle. "What in God's name are you saying? I...that's nonsense. I don't love your sister more than you."

"Yes, you do."

"No, I don't. What kind of father loves his kids unequally?"

She shot him a glare. "Fathers like you. Be like your sister. Your sister did this. She doesn't make me mad. She is this. She is that. That sounds like you. She is the company's president."

Her father's expression blanched. Yes, this was the start she needed. She wasn't going to just endure in silence.

He needs to know what's happening.

"When Aunt Madeline died, I knew how hard it was for Jadesola growing up to not know her mother. I know she was going through a hard time, and I am happy you were there for her. But did you ever stop to think I was struggling, too? You never had time for me."

Her fingers tapped the edge of the chair. A younger image of herself flashed in her head. Those nights of crying as she cuddled Jadesola on her big bed. Her poor sister never understood.

Her father frowned. "She was a young girl then. I just didn't want her to feel bad. You...you were just rebellious in your teenage years, and you were withdrawn."

"Do you know why? I am also sad my mother isn't with me. Popsi, you didn't talk about my mother for years." There was this low feeling down in her stomach. Just talking about it made her mad at her mother.

"You need to calm down. The company has busy staff. Anyone will hear you. I am sure you don't want them talking about your mother." Her father glimpsed at the door.

Iyawa paced her father's office. "I don't care. The problem is why you are so ashamed of her? You are rich. No one cares who you've slept with. You didn't leave you wife for her, so no one can blame you."

"People will call you an illegitimate child. They will call you a bastard who has no mother. I don't want that for you. I don't want them calling you things you are not." Her father sighed. "Ask anyone, no one knows who your mother is. They just have guesses."

Her expression softened a little bit. He didn't want her to be called an illegitimate child? That was sensible. "Why don't you talk about my mother with me instead? Why?"

"I...because she is a one-night-stand, and it almost destroyed my home. Your Aunt Madeline was devastated. I was so ashamed of myself. Talking about her makes me remember how I didn't control myself then."

"And I have to bear the consequences of your actions? I needed a father, too. You followed Jadesola to the shopping mall on her tenth birthday, but you never followed me to one. It was either one of our nannies. Popsi, I don't like the way you treat me."

She didn't want to cry. Not in front of him. It was something she had trained herself to do while growing up.

"I...I didn't know I was doing that. I...you...Iyawa, you need to understand. You were hard training while growing up. I tried my best as a father. You wouldn't listen to anything I say."

She sniffed back tears. "That was because I didn't know about my mother then. I thought you took me away from her."

"I would never have separated you from your mother if she wanted you. She said she had a life to face. You might not believe—"

"I believe. I visited my mother." She was now looking at her boots.

"What?"

She winced. "She lives in South Africa."

"What?"

Her eyebrows shot up. "I said I visited my mother."

"I heard you the first time. Oh, Iyawa. You lied to me?" He rubbed his forehead, groaning.

"Urrmm...you wouldn't talk about her, and I was curious."

"And? What was the outcome?"

"She has new family now."

He nodded. "And what did she say?"

"You were right about her not wanting me, but it doesn't make as a disguise for how you treated me while I was growing up. Yes, I did stupid things, but not because I enjoyed it."

This new information caused him to look at her with burning curiosity.

"Then why?"

"I..." She closed her eyes shut. Why was she telling her father this? "Being wild comforted me in a way. It took my mind off all my worries."

"Iyawa, that is so unhealthy. Why didn't you ever tell me? We could have worked something out, you know. You wouldn't have to be with Matthias right now. I wouldn't have to block your account. I wouldn't have to be so harsh on you."

She grimaced and shrugged.

"You never gave me listening ears. You never did. It was..." She silently apologized to her sister. "I would always say this because it is the truth. I love Jadesola, but...it was all Jadesola. You made me feel left out, so I relied on something else."

"I didn't know I made you feel that way. I can't believe I made you feel you were lesser. You are my first child. I love both my girls equally. I...I think I was distant with you."

"No jokes. You were."

Her father rose from his seat, using his hand to make gestures. "I am sorry, Iyawa. I am sorry about your mother. I am sorry for not being there for you when you needed it. I apologize for being hard on you. I am sorry I made you feel lesser. I am sorry for your account and forcing you on Matthias. I was just a single father trying to do his best."

"It is okay. I...I am not sad or anything. Just wanted to give you a heads up about the whole situation."

She moved towards the door. Should she be relieved? She just had this conversation with her father. Iyawa tried processing her feelings.

"Iyawa."

"Yes, Popsi?"

"I know I don't go out for lunch, but how about we go together?"

"Would Jadesola come along?"

"Only if you want."

She smiled. "Yes. I want Jadesola to come along."

"Iyawa." Her father stopped her again.

"Yes, Father?"

"Let's get you your bank account back." He managed a small smile. "You will have to get a beautiful dress for the launching, anyways."

Iyawa smiled. She was ready to take things slow with her dad.

Chapter Nineteen

With dread, the launching of TeleInc's latest phone came faster than Iyawa expected. She plastered on a smile, staring at the cup of water in her hand. This was it. Last night, she and Matthias had gone to the movies together. After today, he would leave her, and she might never get to tell him how she really felt. If only he just felt what she was feeling.

What if I told him how I felt?

You never know something unless you asked, and if there was something she didn't like, it was cowardice. If he rejected her feelings, it wouldn't be the first time.

From behind, someone coughed. She swivelled around to meet his gaze. He had come to pick her so they could go together. His black suit was on point...and....it seemed he had a new haircut. *God, this man is hot.*

"I knew I was right when I told you red looks good on you. You look astonishing....and you smell nice."

Iyawa was wearing a short ruffled cold-shoulder dress with her latest nude boots. She turned around to meet his gaze.

"I don't usually smell nice?"

He watched her with amusement. "I didn't say that. It is just kind of different. I know what your perfume smells like, and this is so much different. I like it."

She tried not to blush. She had gotten a new perfume at the mall, but he didn't need to know this, right? "I wasn't wearing it for you."

"It is this dress you are wearing for me, then?" He wiggled his eyebrows.

She rolled her eyes. "Shut up. Can we just go now?"

"Yes...I just have something to tell you."

Iyawa's heart skyrocketed for a moment. She wondered what it was, seeing how his face had changed.

She found her voice. "What is it?"

"After the event. I will only tell you after the event." His finger caressed her hand.

She allowed her thoughts to surface again. She wished she could read from his expression.

"Okay. I will wait."

He kissed her forehead. "Let us go. Everyone will be waiting for us."

· · ~ · ·

THE HALL WAS DARK AND cool. Dark as in no lights were switched on, and cool as if the AC was set at the highest degree. Even with the favourable atmosphere, her mind was spinning. Iyawa was seated in the middle of her sister and Matthias, with their father probably standing at the back of the audience watching with pride and delight. Things had been going on pretty well between them. Her father was trying to understand her now, and although it was a cute, small effort, she appreciated him for even trying.

"Why are you restless?" Jadesola asked, her eyebrows drawn in a frown. The bob extension on her hair really made her look like a sexy boss lady.

Iyawa waved her dismissively. "No, I am not. I am just excited about the launch of TeleSpark."

Before she could feed her sister with more lies, Jadesola held up a finger. "You should stop lying. It doesn't fit you."

Matthias's eyes were fixed on his phone, and she could barely see his face. Jadesola seemed to have followed her gaze because she soon felt the warmth of her sister's hand on hers. Iyawa took a deep breath.

"Did he say anything to you?"

"He wants to tell me something after the event," she whispered to her sister. "What if he doesn't love me back? That's all I can think of."

"Then he is missing out on a rare gem. Babe, you need to relax. I can see through your worries. Don't let him see you all stressed like this."

Iyawa nodded. "Thank you. I...I just don't know why, but I feel something is going to go wrong."

"Nothing will go wrong. It is all just in your head."

Just then, white lights came on, and everyone started clapping. The large screen in front of the audience switched on, and with a serene music, began displaying all the TeleInc's gadgets including the TeleSpark phone from TeleSpark 5 to the latest 10.

Iyawa glimpsed Matthias clapping, the light from the screen illuminating his face.

When the screen got hung up on the logo of TeleInc, one of their software engineers came up on stage, and everyone began clapping again. David Jesuloba had been the MC of all TeleInc launching events.

The event got busy with David talking about future TeleSparks and how he was going to tell them about the latest TeleSpark. The screen lit up with six different colours of TeleSpark 10 like black, red, white, pink, purple, and green. David stated its new improved battery life and how it was much slimmer.

"Meet TeleSpark 10. Slim and polished, and also has a stylish design."

David called one of TeleInc researchers to come upstage and talk more about the newly researched apps on TeleSpark 10. It went quickly, with a female software engineer coming up to talk about the TeleSpark 5G network using the screen as her guide. When the engineer was off the stage, David turned to the screen which showed an enlarged image of the phone's dual camera.

"It is your turn now." Jadesola smiled at her. "Go get them to like that camera, baby."

Iyawa breathed in. This was not the first time she was talking in front of a large audience, yet her hands were sweaty.

Matthias placed a hand on her shoulder. "You look uncomfortable. He just called you on stage now. Whatever it is, relax. This would be on TV and screens so do your best."

Some people were now glancing at her. No, no one must see her in this condition. She raised her chin high and smiled.

"I would like to invite Iyawa, the daughter of TeleInc's CEO, to tell us about the improvement in TeleSpark Camera systems," David said again.

Matthias and Jadesola applauded her first, urging her to get to her feet with the audience joining in.

Iyawa rose from her seat and sashayed her way up the stage where she received a mic boom from a technical team. She pushed away her thoughts. There was no way she was going to spoil this. Her family had gone too far for her to mess it up. The confident side of her burst open.

"Good morning, everyone, and welcome to the launching of our latest gadget." She took two steps forward. "We bring you the most advanced TeleSpark. As you all know, we put our customers first. Your satisfaction is our goal. At TeleInc, we strive to give you all better technology."

The screen behind her lit up with yellow labels around TeleSpark 10 dual camera, and everyone applauded again.

"TeleSpark allows you capture high quality images with fifty megapixels."

The image of a beautiful Fulani lady in Fulani attire came on screen. "TeleSpark 10 also allows you the use of optical image stabilization. This is the best camera phone you can get. Trust me, we don't tell lies at TeleInc."

Everyone applauded her as she walked back to her seat. Jadesola made a kissing face. "That was good."

Matthias placed a quick kiss on her lips. It was fast, yet it made her nerves relax. "I am so proud of you."

Just tell me what you want to tell me.

After the launching event had ended, a mini celebration party where everyone was served wine took place. Iyawa stood beside Matthias and Jadesola as everyone was congratulating them.

Her father resurfaced, stretching out his arm. "I am so glad it was a success. Iyawa, you did a great job."

"Hey, Popsi, she deserves a hug," Jadesola said.

Iyawa chuckled, stretching out her hands. "Come in here, Popsi."

Her father tapped her back as she withdrew from the hug. "That was a success. I am proud of you all for making this possible."

"Jaseth," someone called as he walked towards them.

"Daniel. Thank you for being here for the event." Her father forced a smile. In business, there were friends, not so friends, and enemies. Daniel was one of the not-so friends. He was a very big business person who didn't like her father's popularity or even the company.

"I couldn't be anywhere else. I was right in that corner when I heard some things I could not believe could happen."

Iyawa rolled her eyes. She didn't have time for this. "What things, Daniel?"

"The big fat lie. You people have been taking us for a fool."

Her father gave a nervous chuckle and continued. "We assure you everything about TeleSpark is true. Don't bother, Daniel. People are probably saving up money to purchase it."

"I was not talking about the phone. How do you feel lying to everyone about your daughter's engagement, huh?" His voice was purposefully loud and ruthless.

Iyawa turned white. She shifted back, resisting the urge to run. "A...I...What are you talking about?"

She peeked at Matthias who looked stricken, his fists clenched together.

"You have no right to come up here and accuse us, Daniel. That is so wrong. Stop being bitter." Jadesola stepped in front of him, wagging a finger at his face.

This time, guests and staff were now looking at them with curiosity, and murmurs could be heard.

"What are you talking about?" a man from behind asked Daniel.

"Witter's blog just confirmed it now. You can all go check. Apparently, the Jaseths begged the Bades to give in to his demands so he could protect his vile daughter's reputation."

Iyawa thought of a way to cover this up. "That is not true. Stop feeding people with lies."

People were on their phones, and gasps erupted. Iyawa stood there, mouth dropped. This Witter girl had not only managed to expose the whole thing but made her family look bad. How did anyone even hear of this? Just her family and Matthias's knew of this.

Iyawa wondered how her father still managed to keep his face in check. Hers had shown all the stages of shock and shame.

"Who is this Witter blog? Is it a verified source?"

Daniel gave a wicked smile. "That doesn't mean it isn't true, Jaseth. Witter's blog has been serving us with real news that has not been called false. Now, how about you also explain that your daughter is an illegitimate child?"

"I am not an illegitimate child. How dare you?"

"You are an illegitimate child, isn't that true? No wonder his real daughter is the company's president."

"Don't you dare talk about her this way." Matthias almost lunged at Daniel.

"Poor man. They forced you into this, didn't they? I knew it was too good to be true. How could someone as wayward as her get a man like Matthias Bade?" A woman spat in disgust.

Murmurs surrounded the room again.

"I was actually surprised she could get any man. I mean, the lady got no self-respect." Another man flared a glare at her.

"Her mother doesn't want her? Like mother, like daughter."

"Matthias doesn't deserve someone like this."

"She could never get a good man. I am so happy Witter made us realize the truth."

Everyone's voices whirled in her head, making her hold her sister for support. *Who did this?* No one else knew about her secrets except her family and Matthias's.

"Jadesola, get Matthias and Iyawa back to the car. Now," her father said.

She couldn't just go like this. It wasn't possible. She had to tell the truth, and she had to tell it in a way that showed Matthias those three months were the best months of her life.

"Fine, you are right. Your stupid Witter's blog is right." Iyawa withdrew from Jadesola's hold.

Her father reached for her. "You don't have to, dear. They will never see things from our perspective."

"No. I do need to talk. Everything is right, but my father didn't beg Matthias." She paused to look at Matthias, pleading silently for him to confirm. But instead, his gaze was downwards. "It was a mutual business thing. Actually, his father was in—"

"Iyawa, stop."

She looked at him, but he avoided her gaze. What was he saying? It was time to tell the world the truth. "I just—"

"I said, stop. Say nothing, please."

The crowd erupted into more accusations and gasps.

"What?"

She gave a dry chuckle. "I...I don't understand. You know we shouldn't live a lie if we want to move forward in our relationship."

"No. Everything we had together was your dad's plan."

"Matthias!"

It was Jadesola who exclaimed because she was too shocked to give him a reply. This Matthias standing in front of her was different from the person she had fallen in love with.

Daniel laughed. A wicked kind of laugh. "You see. Not every rich person is a good person. I always knew there was something fishy about the engagement."

Iyawa wanted to reach out to Matthias. Her brain could not differentiate right from wrong, and it seemed like everything was just too much.

"Matthias, I have a question. W...what about...all the time we spent together? Was it all because of my dad?" She couldn't even form her words right. Everyone was now shaking heads at her, giving her those looks of disdain and pity.

Silence sprinkled its dust in the environment as everyone waited for him to reply.

"Those feelings. That excitement. You felt it, too, Matthias. Please say something."

She knew she was being desperate, but she just wanted him to talk, to tell everyone their relationship might have been a lie, but he had fallen in love with her.

"Iyawa, *Abeg. May we comot for here.*" Jadesola pulled her away.

"Speak up, Matthias! You said we have a connection we should explore!"

She took a glimpse at his face. He swallowed hard and met her gaze. It was like he was pleading for her to play along.

Realization suddenly hit her. He didn't want anyone to know about his father's debt. How could she play along to such a thing? Still, a part of her wondered how he could stand there and lie to everyone to save his face.

Her father shook his head at Matthias. "This is absurd. You care to explain why—"

Iyawa held her father's hand. "No. It is okay. Let us just go."

Two bodyguards came and took her away from the scene. Iyawa didn't bother looking at Matthias, and she didn't even resist being taken away.

So this is what heartbreak feels like?

It felt like her heart was shattering into tiny pieces of glass that couldn't be reglued. Iyawa doubted if her heart would ever heal from this or if she would ever see Matthias again.

Chapter Twenty

@taiyecrotchet_naija
Nawa ooo! Celebrities in Nigeria are already spoiling this world ooo. How you go do fake engagement to save your ass?
@funmijolomijuwonbella
No be today life don dey spoil. Just look at how Iyawa tried covering up her bad image.
@Alhajamemunat556 replied:
As in. It is very wrong when Nigerians try copying celebrities overseas. I am just 😳. May Allah let her find someone else that will overlook her past because she is trending now.
@b.o.l.a.n.leer
This Iyawa story is teaching we ladies to carry ourselves with dignity. Past will always come to eat you up. I feel for her sha. She looks like she is in love with the guy.

Iyawa squirmed on her bed, sipping from her cup of coffee. She had managed to get through the week, bottled up in her room. It wasn't long before her Popsi and his agent found the culprit. The brain behind the whole chaos was a female staff Iyawa could have sworn she had never seen before. She didn't even know many staff. The lady had listened to Iyawa and Popsi's talk the day after she arrived back in Nigeria. The staff was fired. Popsi threatened to sue Witter's blog if she didn't take down her post. Witter, being the smart lady she was, took it down.

Iyawa thought this would help, but social media would not forget it.

"Please go on. There must be more."

"That's all."

"Jadesola, those are just three tweets. I trust Naija Twitter—never gonna call it X; it would be more than this."

Iyawa was familiar with the platform and its algorithms. Her mind went back to the time a popular social media influencer's sex tape was released. Naija Twitter didn't let the matter rest. The sex tape was an unwelcomed visitor on every blog she visited.

Jadesola turned to look at her, hands on her hips. "I am not reading you any more tweets. Twitter is not that important when it comes to trendy news."

"You know that's not true."

"It is the truth. This, too, will fade away. Besides, you haven't done anything that bad." Jadesola slumped on the bed next to her.

"I faked being engaged to a guy who lied to the whole world to protect his stupid reputation. That is news-worthy, and it won't fade away."

Matthias's actions peaked her anger once again. She reflected with bitterness on how he'd looked away from her and told that lie to the whole world. Iyawa cradled her mug and sipped her coffee again.

"God. I wish I can take back my words about Matthias. I thought he was like Benjy."

Iyawa ignored his name, resisting the urge to think about him. He wasn't going to take a rent-free space in her mind.

"How many Youtube views? I need to know how famous I am now."

"I don't know."

"Just tell me."

"I told you, it is not important."

"Just say it, Jadesola. You know I can always check, right?"

Her sister groaned. "I will just give you a hint. Six."

"Sixty thousand?" She licked her lips with hope. Not so bad.

Jadesola dropped her lashes quickly, and Iyawa caught on. "Jadesola, is it six hundred thousand?"

"No. Six million views, but I swear it doesn't matter."

She tried swallowing the lump lingering in her throat. She was everywhere. Getting to her feet, she dropped her mug on the bedside table.

"I want to know more, please. Am I on Instagram? Please, let me know."

"No, Iyawa. You shouldn't be healing by reading these trolls tweets and stupid views. This is insane." Jadesola dropped her phone to the bed. "Something is different, though."

Iyawa threw her hands in distress. "What?"

"I know my sister. She is badass. Iyawa, you don't normally care about the news and stuffs. What is happening?"

The torment in her heart plagued her like a disease. Her head was down, her body shaking in misery. She closed her eyes, but images of Matthias made her open them again. "I don't know. I...I am just angry, I guess."

"Or you are hurting because the one you loved didn't love you back." Jadesola stood up and walked to where she was standing. "I know how you feel."

Swallowing the sob threatening to come out, she looked up. "I...I just can't believe what's happening. I can't stop thinking of what he wanted to tell me that night. He didn't want people to ridicule his family because they are in debt, but he just ridiculed my love for him."

"Oh. I am sorry you feel this way. When you love someone, you yearn for them. They cloud your every thought and make your heart race at every second. So, it is understandable when you realized all of it was just an illusion. Something you were just seeing because you wanted to see it. Iyawa, allow yourself to feel everything you think you need to feel. Time is the best healer."

Her sister was right. Matthias never said he loved her. He only felt they had a connection and needed to explore it. Perhaps he realized he couldn't be with someone like her. Someone as dirty as she was. No one wanted to be with someone with a past like hers, and she understood it.

"I don't just understand. I...Why give me all those cute kisses only to break my heart? I wanted to change. All my life, I thought being wild was an escape route for me, and heaven knows, I wanted to change. Not for him, but for myself. I thought it would be a bonus if he realized I didn't live this kind of life again. I even planned on going to a therapist to help me deal with these things."

"Iyawa, you will be fine. This is all because of that stupid Witter's blog. You know, I love how Popsi told her never to write of us again. Why do people care about what you do with your life, anyways?" Jadesola just stood there, breathless with anger. "Hey, why don't we go do something different tomorrow? I don't think it would be easy convincing you today, so what do you say?"

Iyawa gave her sister an incredulous look. "We are not going shopping in the midst of crisis. Let us just order takeaway this night and binge on that new Netflix series."

"C'mon. I don't want to watch the new series. There is chaos already. Just imagine how badass we would be going to the gym in the midst of all this chaos. You love being the badass queen."

"The gym? No. Thank you." Her mind flashed to the image of Matthias in the gym. No. No thoughts of that man again. "Besides, we have a gym here."

Jadesola gave her the puppy face. "Iyawa, come on. Our gym is small. You know we've always wanted to work out and get all sweaty. We will take a picture and post on Instagram. I know you love things like that. I'll book us an appointment. Please say yes! Say yes!"

Iyawa resisted the urge to roll her eyes. The idea sounded tempting. She would love to relax and work out instead of staying locked up in her room worried about the number of views and tweets. She had dealt with being the trending news in the past, and she was going to deal with this, too.

She pulled Jadesola's nose playfully. "You already plan to book us an appointment, how can I say no?"

"Yay! That's awesome."

"You know what else is awesome?"

Jadesola pulled on a questioning gaze. "I don't think I do."

"You are," she said with a smile.

. . ∞ . .

IYAWA ROLLED HER EYES at the exaggerated heavy breathings and grunts of the men in the gym. The place was quite different from what she'd expected it to be. It had this weird mixture of sweat and deodorant and also had glass walls and numerous machines she couldn't name.

She got on the treadmill next to Jadesola who was wearing a brown tank top now soaked in sweat even with the breeze oozing from the air conditioners.

"What were you doing?" Jadesola asked.

"I was warming up my muscles." Iyawa gave her sister an up-and-down stare. "What in the earth? You just got on the machine."

"I...I can't even catch my breath. Am I going too fast?"

She glanced at the machine. "I don't know. Are you?"

"What should I do? This is not fun."

"This is a fitness centre. Not an amusement park, Jadesola. Please, don't die on me. This was your idea."

"I know, right. If only there was something interesting to watch." Jadesola gasped at something behind Iyawa and quickly put off the machine. "Look at that man helping that woman. I think he is a trainer."

Iyawa turned to look at the dark-brown-skinned man feet away from them, helping a woman with a machine that kind of pushed her leg front and back. She could not deny the man was extremely handsome. He was wearing a red sweat-shirt with cuffed jog pants. She ignored the little part of her wanting to compare him to Matthias.

This is not about him.

Iyawa set the machine to a light run and put in her ear pods. "So, what about him? He works at the gym."

"He is hot. Just look at all those biceps threatening to come out of that sweat shirt. Look." Jadesola pointed at the man, her mouth twisting into a mischievous smile.

Just then, the man caught Iyawa and Jadesola staring and waved at them. Jadesola waved back, and Iyawa tried not to slap her hard. She didn't like when men caught her staring. It made them have a kind of ego she didn't like.

"He is not my type. I don't even have a type. If you don't mind now, I am going to reach for my phone and play me a nice song."

Minutes later, the same gym man approached them, his face packed in a smile. Iyawa groaned inwardly and took a peek at Jadesola who shot her a don't-you-dare look.

Iyawa forced her lips to give in to a smile and removed her ear pods. She got why Jadesola wanted her to mingle with men, but she didn't want to.

The man stood tall with his hands in his pocket. "Hi, pretty ladies. The name is Dabira."

"I am Jadesola, and this is my sister, Iyawa. This is our first time working out together. We rarely visit the gym," Jadesola said in a saccharine tone.

"We have a gym. She is lying."

Jadesola rolled her eyes. "She is boring."

"Really? One would never tell just by looking at both of you." Dabira turned to meet her gaze. "You look so focused. Welcome to Chefa's fitness centre."

Arghh. He was flirting.

"Is there anything I can help you both with, or do you plan on using the treadmill alone?"

Iyawa shrugged. "I don't know. What do you have in mind for us?"

"There are machines I can help you with." He rested his elbow on the treadmill. "And if you want, we have dumbbells."

"Those weighty things, huh?"

Iyawa sighed. "Jadesola, no one calls it weighty things."

"I am now." She scoffed.

"You ladies want to try out the weighty things? If yes, follow me."

If Jadesola was going, she was also going. Dabira took them to a weight bench and asked Iyawa to lay on it. After he helped her with weights, he complimented her strength and stamina.

Iyawa sat up on the weight bench, still smiling at Dabira's comment. It was then her soul flew out of her body when she saw Matthias standing metres away from her. He was wearing a sweaty tank top and shorts, a water bottle in his hand. They both froze like icebergs, staring at each other like they had never seen one another before.

Jadesola followed her gaze and held her arm. "Are you okay? We could leave if you want us to."

"No. It is just Matthias. He is of no harm."

He was still as handsome as she remembered. His dark eyes travelled from her face to Jadesola's and to Dabira at her back. There was a hint of sadness on his face when he looked at her again, and she felt that overwhelming power to reach out to him.

It was then she realized how much she missed him. Would he speak to her? Would he approach her and apologize for what he did? A part of her knew she was going to forgive him if he walked up to her.

To her surprise, he did not approach her. Instead, he continued his walk ahead, and she watched him stroll out of the gym. Iyawa ached with another inner pain.

Her sister hugged her, placing a soft kiss on her forehead. "I am so sorry. I swear, I didn't know he was going to be here."

"Of course, you couldn't have known. This gym is for everyone. It is not like his name was stamped on the building." Her sentence, which was meant to bring humour, lacked laughter.

"I don't know what just happened now, but I would understand if you need to go." Dabira stood from his knees, his feet ready to walk away.

Iyawa held his hand. "Do not go. I would still love to try more exercises."

"Are you sure, Im? We could go shopping or have smoothies. Anything," Jadesola said.

"I want to stay here. Besides, it is only Matthias."

She repeated it like it was some mantra that would calm her nerves down. It was only Matthias, and yet, she wasn't interested in the gym anymore.

· · ❧ · ·

WHEN JADESOLA'S CAR passed beside the familiar black vehicle in front of their aluminium gate, Iyawa's legs grew weak. It wasn't until the gateman opened the gate and their car drove in that her suspicion was confirmed. Matthias was leaning on the left white pillars of the white building, pressing a phone.

Iyawa checked if she could still breathe again. He was still wearing his gym outfit. Her mind raced with different questions. What was he doing here? Was he looking for her? Surely, it was her. She doubted her sister or Popsi wanted to see him now.

"Did you know he was coming here?" Jadesola asked her, releasing her seat belt, her eyes still fixed on the man in front of her.

By this time, Matthias had noticed their car. He waved awkwardly.

"No. I didn't know he was even going to be here. I haven't been talking to him."

"Do you want me to send him away? I can tell the guards to throw him out or whatever you want. It is okay if you don't want to see him yet."

Iyawa managed a smile. "I am fine, Jadesola. Just go inside. I will meet him."

"Will you be fine? You know you don't have to listen to a word he says."

"I know, but I want to."

"Be good."

Iyawa remained in her seat. Jadesola got out of the car and approached the building, not without stopping by and muttering some words to Matthias that made his face pale.

When her sister was gone, Iyawa got down from the car. Matthias halted in front of her. Being so close to him, she realized she missed him.

"Hey. I didn't know you had dogs," he said.

She felt a twinge in her knee. Surely, those couldn't be his first words to her. "Dogs?"

"Jadesola threatened to throw me to the dogs if I hurt you again."

"I would say don't underestimate her. She could get dogs, you know," she answered him sharply.

"I will keep that in mind."

A look of sadness washed over his face, and she almost reached out to cup his cheeks.

"I am sure you are not here to talk about Jadesola and dogs. Is there something else?" she asked.

"No. It's not why I am here."

"Then why are you here?"

Matthias's throat seemed to close because it took seconds before he answered. "I miss you, Iyawa. I tried calling you, but you wouldn't pick up, and I understand why. But when I saw you at the gym, I...couldn't stop thinking about you."

"What do you want, Matthias? You can't just come here saying these things to me." Iyawa paused, her torment almost taking over. "It is not right. Please leave."

"Iyawa, I am sorry."

"For what, exactly? For spoiling my family name and saving yours?" Could she even look at him and not feel such misery?

Matthias's voice was filled with suffering. "I didn't mean for this to happen. Iyawa, my father is a fragile soul. If the whole world knows he is in debt, I doubt if he can take it."

"So you just wanted to be the saint? The guy who helps his family? It wasn't yours to decide who to save. We could have told the whole world what happened, and we could have gone through it together."

"I can't do that to my father. Yours has been popular with the media. I just thought your father would always come out of these things like he always did."

It was like someone had slapped her on the cheeks.

"Well, I am sorry my family isn't as normal as yours. Why are you even here? Your father is saved, and the Jaseths are the devils now. You should be hosting a party for it."

"If only it was simple. I am here because I wanted to see you again." He took deep breaths. "I missed everything about you. I can't stop thinking about you. You know that day, I wanted to tell you—"

"Get out. I don't want to hear it. Deep down, you are ashamed of me. I understand if you don't want to be associated with someone who like me. It is totally human, but do not tell me lies."

"I have never judged your past," he said

"What you did that night was worse than any judgement you could have given me. You took me out of a scandal and threw me into a bigger one. Everyone is saying my name. I am the one who fell in love with a good guy who doesn't want me. That is the story outside." Iyawa fumed.

"What should I do to fix everything?"

She looked at him. There was only one thing he could do.

"Let everyone know the truth."

"Iyawa—"

"Just tell everyone the truth. Let them know why we had this fake engagement in the first place." She hated how desperate she was now.

Matthias's shoulders slumped. "I am sorry, Iyawa. My father—"

That was it. He wasn't going to say the truth. Her body trembled with the possibility he might never choose her.

"Don't call me or text me again. I don't want to see you or hear your name."

He could have fixed things between them when he had the chance, but he was still happy being the coward guy. If he didn't want her, then so be it. She would survive without Matthias.

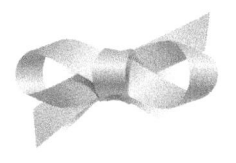

Chapter Twenty-One

The room was a big one and a very calm space. Pictures were on the wall, and bookshelves could be seen the behind the lady. A desk also sat in the room, placed on a beautiful rug. A pleasant aroma in the space made her relax.

Iyawa shifted on the big couch, exploring the office of her new therapist.

"Miss Jaseth," the older woman, Dr Lade Akintobi, said. Her black hair with grey strands was packed into a bun, making her look pretty.

After researching and asking around, Iyawa and Jadesola had finally chosen a therapist in Ikorodu. Besides, Ikorodu was just an hour's journey away from Ikeja. This morning, her Popsi had taken a day off work and brought her down to the therapist's office with Jadesola seated beside him. Iyawa didn't know how to feel. Her whole family supporting her really made her heart leap for joy.

"Be good. Just call us when you are done. We are taking this car on a little stroll," he had told her.

Her father was trying to fix their relationship, and she was grateful.

"It is okay if you don't want to answer the question. I just wanted to know what event brought you here so I can understand the problem." Dr Lade smiled at her.

"Wait, what's that smell?"

"Lavender. You like it?" Dr Lade asked.

Iyawa nodded. The therapist had asked why she was seeking therapy. The answer was simple, but this was the first time she had to put a term to what was happening with her.

"I...I have this compulsive behaviour, and I think I need help. I need a safe place where I can't be judged." Iyawa looked at her therapist. "Where...I...I can't feel ashamed."

Iyawa knew probably all therapist were nice, but Dr Lade sometimes laughed to her jokes, and it made her feel relaxed. There were some questions she didn't want to answer, and the woman was understanding. She went on to asking questions like what Iyawa expected of this therapy and went on discussing something she called strategies.

It sounded like a lot of work, and not a day or session would pass without her having to talk about her mother or even Matthias, but she was ready to do the work.

·· ❦ ··

IYAWA PULLED OUT HER phone and pressed it to her left ear. She was standing in front of her therapist's building, waiting for Jadesola and her Popsi to come pick her up. The road was bustling with people in formal attire walking down the road and a few cars and *Okada*s driving by.

She's thought after the session, she was supposed to see changes. Rather, she was feeling uncomfortable and exposed.

"Hello."

"Iyawa, are you done?" Jadesola's voice on the other end said. "Should we come now?"

"Yeah." She could hear slight munching in the background. She should have known Jadesola would never joke with her tummy. "Are you eating?"

Jadesola chuckled. "Mmm...yes. I only had tea this morning. Even Popsi is mauling on a donut now."

"Really? I can't believe you guys thought it was right to have snacks without getting mine." She feigned offence.

"We got you a donut and scotch egg, of course." Before Iyawa could thank her sister, she heard Jadesola say, "Hey Popsi, you've spilled jam on your shirt."

"Popsi got jam on his shirt? Are you kidding me?"

"Have I ever joked about something like this? There is colour on his shirt." Jadesola was now laughing hard, joy rumbling in her laughter.

"Take a picture."

"No, do not take a picture," her father protested.

"I need a picture. I haven't had a good laugh since forever." Iyawa shifted the phone to her other ear. She was drowning in a pit of satisfaction and blissfulness. The problem was how a part of her wanted Matthias to be a part of it.

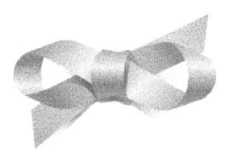

Chapter Twenty-Two

Yam porridge with *Ponmos* covered in rich red stew. The perfect food to have when you were sitting alone at a table in the office cafeteria. She had just resumed work. After those long, depressing days at home, she'd decided it was time to get her feet outside.

Iyawa dug her fork into the porridge, savouring the sweet taste. Staff were still peeking at her like she was some sort of injured chicken. Social apps seemed to have forgotten about her, but people still loved to take a glimpse. These people were her employees, for crying out loud.

She met the eyes of the green-robed waitress, offering her a smirk. The waitress scrambled away, pretending to clear up the dishes. Iyawa shook her head. People could be really funny.

"I am so angry, I want to throw your plate away. Wait, is that porridge?" Jadesola asked, taking a seat in front of her.

Iyawa repositioned her plate away from her sister. "Yes, it is porridge. If you do anything to my porridge, I will kill you before I ask you what's wrong with you."

"I can't believe you. You are supposed to be caring."

"I was planning to. Until you threatened to throw away my lunch. What got you all riled up, anyways?"

"Benjamin." Jadesola slouched.

Iyawa wished her sister could get a beautiful love story where Benjy would love her.

"Argghhhh. Benjamin again. I have heard this guy's name more than his family has. What is up?" Her brows puckered.

"Stop groaning. I like him, okay?"

"I know you do. You've been talking about him ever since he gave you that stupid birthday card. I just don't get why you can't tell him how you feel."

"I can't. You know I can't."

Iyawa leaned forward, her elbows on the table. "Why?"

"It is too risky. What if he rejects me?"

"That is the only extreme thing that could happen. Rejection doesn't kill. Take it from me."

Jadesola drew her mouth into a straight line. "It will kill me if it comes from Benjy. I love him. I want him to see more than just Mr Jaseth's younger daughter. When you love someone, you want them to feel you as much as you feel them."

"I know. But the poor guy doesn't know you love him. Tell him. He might also love you, you know. Some guys are shy." She shoved another forkful of yam porridge into her mouth.

"I will try. I am still gathering the courage. Please, is this how love feels? So beautiful and yet frustrating." Jadesola's gaze seemed to stray from her and to something behind her.

Iyawa turned her head. A younger lady pretty much the age of Jadesola was approaching them. Only she was running.

"Jen, why are you running?" Jadesola asked, patting to the seat next to her.

Jen placed her hand on the table like it was to help steady her breath. "You've got to see this, Shar."

"Shar?" Iyawa didn't think Jadesola's name could be shortened for a nickname, not until she met Jen.

"Oh, Iyawa. Meet Jennifer. Our social media manager. She is a friend of mine."

The idea of Jadesola having a new friend made her a little jealous. Jadesola was her only friend.

Jen stretched her hand to shake Iyawa. "Hey, Miss Iyawa. Wow, this is the first time I am talking to you face to face."

"Jen. You wanted to show me something," Jadesola said.

Jen nodded, handing over her phone to Jadesola. "Look at this. This is Instagram Live."

Iyawa tried paying attention to her food. Seeing the younger ladies talk about Instagram made her feel like she had to make new friends.

"Oh my God. How did you see this?" Jadesola asked.

"He is live."

Jennifer was now looking at her. Iyawa didn't know why, and she kind of didn't want to find out.

"Iyawa, have you checked your phone today? I mean your Instagram."

"I hate Instagram. What is it?" She was curious, seeing the change on Jadesola's face.

Jadesola turned the phone directly at her. "It is Matthias."

Her stomach clenched. She stared speechlessly at the phone. Matthias's dark eyes seemed like they were staring at her. He looked like he hadn't been getting enough rest, but he could still charm her with that face.

"I am sorry for what I did. I hurt the Jaseths with my lies. What happened between us was truly an agreement between the two families. The reason I lied was because...I...I...I didn't want anyone to know about my father's huge debt. Mr Jaseth promised to pay it up if I faked being engaged to his daughter, and I did it because of money."

Jadesola reached for her hand. "Iyawa, are you okay?"

Was she okay? She didn't even know. Matthias was here telling the whole world about her father's debt. Comments were rolling in underneath the video.

I can't believe he lied.

God, he is so cute.

Love emojis

That Iyawa girl is a devil

I don't believe anything

"I faked being engaged to her, not because her father threatened me, but because we wanted him to pay our debts. Iyawa, I am sorry. I am sorry I care about what people think. Those days we spent together, hating each other, frustrating one another. It wasn't easy faking things at first, but you know, we got better at it."

She was barely able to keep the heat from radiating from her body.

"Things changed, Iyawa. Things changed when I stopped everything to look at you laugh. It was as if your laughter controlled my breathing. Things changed when I took a moment to admire you while your feet burnt in hot oil."

"You burnt your feet?" Jadesola asked.

"Yeah, shhh."

"Things changed when I couldn't stop thinking of you. Things changed for me when we kissed. Things changed when Google got tired of me searching 'how to confess your love to a woman.'" Matthias was laughing in a gentle manner.

"Get to the point, son. You might be boring her already," a familiar voice said.

A small laugh floated from her throat. She couldn't believe his mother was there, too.

"I like the way you make me feel. In your absence, you still have a control on me. I don't care about your past. It is meaningless to me. I don't care about what anyone has to say. I miss you, Iyawa. *Te Amo*."

His eyes were so compelling, she wished she could hug him through the screen.

The camera shuffled, and Ifeoma's face came on. "Hey, Iyawa. If you are listening to this, my brother is in front of the restaurant where he fake-proposed to you. If you love him, come meet him here. If you don't, well, he deserves it for what he did to you. I am sorry for everything."

"Iyawa. Do you want to—"

"What are you even asking? That was the most romantic Instagram Live ever. Yes, she wants to go. Sorry, do you want to go?" Jennifer said with dreamy eyes.

It was at this moment she approved of Jennifer's friendship with her sister.

"Yes. I love him. Jadesola, you drive this time. I have to go see Matthias." Her senses leapt with a new heart. She loved him.

The drive to the restaurant was going to take about thirty minutes, and that's if they were fortunate to not encounter traffic. She took a deep breath and restricted herself from chewing on her finger.

"Could you drive any faster?" Jennifer asked from her place in the passenger's seat.

"Jen. This is a car. Not an airplane," Jadesola hissed.

Iyawa wished the car could fly.

"Jen, is he still live?" Iyawa asked.

Jen checked her phone. "No. He is no longer live. I bet he is still at the restaurant."

The car finally parked at a lane opposite the restaurant. She could see Matthias's car, and this alone got her jumping out of her sister's car.

Matthias was leaning on his car, with his sister and mother inside. He was wearing a polo-shirt and dark jeans with black shades on. He had a way of taking her breath away.

"Iyawa. You came." He took off his shades like they didn't allow him to see well.

She ambled towards him. "I want to slap you. I really wanna slap you so hard."

"Please do. Slap me. I deserve everything, I hurt you." He took her face in his hands, pulling her to him.

She removed his hands. "Yes, you did. You broke my heart. I was miserable, you know."

"I am sorry. I couldn't stop thinking about you. So please, slap me."

"I will. After you kiss me."

"I promise to kiss you, but first, do you love me?"

"Stupid. If I didn't love you, I wouldn't be here. I left a yam porridge for you. Yes, I love you. I love you so much."

His hands slipped behind her neck, and his lips placed a quick kiss on her forehead, cheeks, and nose. When he stared at her lips, she couldn't resist from asking.

"Why do you always do that? You kiss my whole face before you kiss me."

"I guess I don't want to miss a thing when I am kissing my whole world."

And then, his mouth met hers with burning necessity, stirring up a sweetness in her. Matthias kissed her like he knew what he had missed. There was this warmth with their kiss that made her knees weaken. Love flew in her like falling rose petals.

"I love you, Matthias. I really do," she said when they withdrew. "Was this what you wanted to tell me that night?"

"Yes. I had planned to tell you so much that night, and I...I chickened out because of what people would say about my father."

"I forgive you. How is your father feeling about all this?" Her own father didn't even know she was out here with Matthias.

"A little sore that I had to tell everyone about his debt, but he is good."

Iyawa turned to his car and saw his sister waving at her. She waved back. His mother simply gave her a smile. "I see your mother in the car. Does she like me now?"

"What if I say she was the one who called me a chicken for not being able to confess my feelings?"

"I like her, then."

He pulled away strands of hair from her face. "Does this mean you are mine now?"

"I am standing here after such a kiss, and you are still asking. Of course I am yours." She gave him an affectionate smile. "You know what that means?"

"That I get to be around you all day and watch you laugh?"

She chuckled. "Yes. It also means you belong to only me."

"I don't think that would be a problem. A world where you and I don't belong to one another?" Matthias shuddered like he'd just woken up from a nightmare. "I don't want to be in that type of world.

She pulled him down for another kiss, savouring this feeling of satisfaction.

Matthias was right. She couldn't think of a world where she didn't have him. As they stood there perfectly still, surrounded by families and passersby, Iyawa tried to breathe. While their breaths mingled with the other, she found herself able to breathe again. Her favourite place to be in the world was in his arms, and she would die there if she had to.

THE END

Thank you for reading Schemes 'N Love by Jomi Oyel. If you enjoyed this story, leave a brief review on the site of purchase and tell a friend/share on social media if you can. For updates on upcoming book releases, sign up to our newsletter: https://www.loveafricapress.com/newsletter

Other books by Jomi Oyel

Love on a Mission
Let the Heart Beat

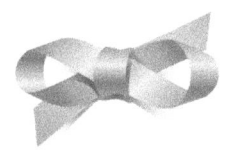

OTHER BOOKS BY LOVE AFRICA PRESS

Locked In by Opemipo Omosa
How to Fix a Broken Heart by Bambo Deen
Love Prey by Tidimalo Motukwa
Amber Fire by Aminat Sanni-Kamal
Against the Run of Play by Kiru Taye
Like Whirlwind by Feyi Aina

CONNECT WITH US
Facebook.com/LoveAfricaPress
Twitter.com/LoveAfricaPress
Instagram.com/LoveAfricaPress
www.loveafricapress.com[1]

---

1. http://www.loveafricapress.com

Milton Keynes UK
Ingram Content Group UK Ltd.
UKHW041220021124
450589UK00005B/499

9 781914 226625